Dayanara

To:

~~Meg, Ben, and Kate~~ my mom

From:

~~Nana~~ Dayanara

Date: 2-1-2014

~~Merry Christmas! 2008~~

I love all of you

very much!

Nana

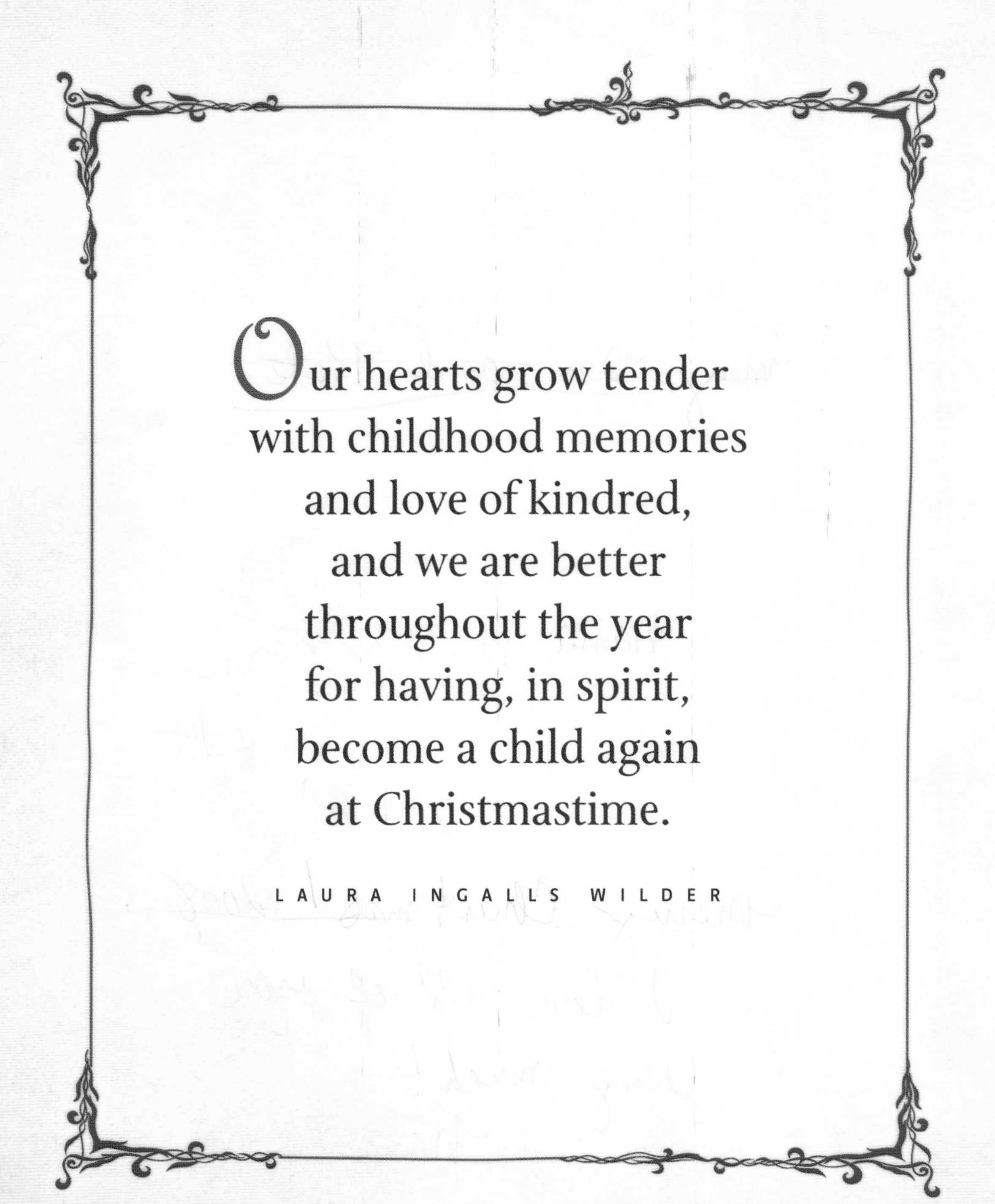

Our hearts grow tender
with childhood memories
and love of kindred,
and we are better
throughout the year
for having, in spirit,
become a child again
at Christmastime.

LAURA INGALLS WILDER

THE Candle IN THE Forest

AND OTHER Christmas Stories CHILDREN LOVE

COMPILED & EDITED BY

JOE WHEELER

Our purpose at Howard Books is to:

- *Increase faith* in the hearts of growing Christians
- *Inspire holiness* in the lives of believers
- *Instill hope* in the hearts of struggling people everywhere

Because He's coming again!

Published by Howard Books, a division of Simon & Schuster, Inc.
1230 Avenue of the Americas, New York, NY 10020
www.howardpublishing.com

Library of Congress Cataloging-in-Publication Data

The candle in the forest : and other Christmas stories children love / compiled and edited by Joe L. Wheeler.
p. cm.
Summary: An illustrated collection of eight children's stories selected for capturing the magic of Christmas along with its true meaning.
1. Christmas stories, American. 2. Children's stories, American. [1. Christmas—Fiction. 2. Christian life—Fiction. 3. Short stories.] I. Wheeler, Joe L., 1936–
PZ5.C16818 2007
[Fic]—dc22
2007014977

ISBN 13: 978-1-4165-4219-3
ISBN 10: 1-4165-4219-1
ISBN 13: 978-1-58229-707-1 (gift edition)
ISBN 10: 1-58229-707-X (gift edition)

10 9 8 7 6 5 4 3 2 1

Manufactured in China

Edited by Chrys Howard
Cover and interior design by Greg Jackson, Thinkpen Design, LLC, www.thinkpendesign.com
Illustrations by Kyle Henry

ACKNOWLEDGMENTS

"The Candle in the Forest," by Temple Bailey. Included in Bailey's collection, *The Holly Hedge and Other Christmas Stories*, Penn Publishing Company, Philadelphia, 1925.

"The Last Straw," by Paula McDonald. Copyright 1992. Reprinted by permission of Covenant Communications, Inc.

"The Tallest Angel," author unknown. If anyone can provide knowledge of the author of this old story, the author's next of kin, or its original publication, please send this information to Joe Wheeler (P.O. Box 1246, Conifer, Colorado 80433).

"The Night My Father Came Home," author unknown. If anyone can provide knowledge of the author of this old story, the author's next of kin, or its original publication, please send this information to Joe Wheeler (P.O. Box 1246, Conifer, Colorado 80433).

"Kitten of Bethlehem," by Ruth C. Ikerman. Published in December 1973 Sunshine Magazine. Reprinted by permission of Garth Heinrich, longtime publisher of *Sunshine Publications*.

"Trouble at the Inn," by Dina Donohue. Reprinted by permission from *Guideposts*. Copyright 1966 by Guideposts, Carmel, New York 10512. All rights reserved.

"A Certain Small Shepherd," by Rebecca Caudill, copyright 1965 by Rebecca Caudill, c 1993 by Rebecca Jean Baker.

"The Red Mittens," by Hartley F. Dailey. Reprinted by permission of Jeanne E. Dailey Sutton.

Table of Contents

The Stories of Christmas
CHILDREN AND CHRISTMAS STORIES

JOSEPH LEININGER WHEELER

"Daddy, is Christmas almost here?"
"No, Dear—it's a long way off yet."
Sigh. "How long is that, Daddy?"

To a child, no other event is comparable to Christmas. New Year's Day, Presidents' Day, St. Patrick's Day, Memorial Day, Fourth of July, Veteran's Day—none of these register in a child's life. Valentine's Day, Easter, and Thanksgiving register, but only a little more. Even birthdays last but a day.

So Christmas stands alone as the most anticipated holiday of the year. And rightly so—it contains that magical combination of fantasy and family. Just saying words such as "manger," "Bethlehem," "reindeer," "candy canes," and "Santa," wafts even the most troubled children to a place they feel was created just for them.

Our own grandchildren come to what we call to our "Electronically Free Grey House" for Christmas. Even before we wake up, they'll crawl in beside us and wiggle and talk and cajole until we get up. Then they'll pounce, begging that we play a game with them. Our electronic equipment ban has blessed us by knowing that while they're with us, our time is theirs, without reservations. And they love it! No amount of electronic anything can possibly compare to having Grammy and Poppy all to themselves.

We enter the world of children, by invitation only, of course, for we no longer belong there.

> *Children . . . , with the dew of heaven scarcely dry on their wings and eyes and ears that still can see and hear, tread sweet wild ways and have no words to tell of them. When they have learnt to pick and choose a telling word and a descriptive phrase the wings have fallen from their shoulders and the old ways are closed. Age has little left to tell of but memories and the trembling hope of returning one day to the old paths.*
>
> ELIZABETH GOUDGE, *Island Magic*

And Christmas is the best of times to enter in; the entrance to this great adventure being only a story away. In fact, a story is like a magic key waiting to open the door to imagination filled with life and love and adventure. For a child and an adult, Story often provides a bridge for the two generations to better understand each other, empathize with each other.

When our children were small, I was privileged, through Story, to briefly enter the magical world they lived in. Then they grew up and moved on, but now that we have grandchildren I am rediscovering that world all over again.

I think what surprises me most about a child's world was expressed best by Elizabeth Goudge in *The Scent of Water:*

"In a child's life there are no empty spaces."

How very true, even more today! A child's life is every bit as full as are ours—even their joys and sorrows are proportional to ours. Once upon a time, every child had a chance to explore the world of imagination. A place and a time when dreams could germinate, sprout, and grow. It was a serene world—until electricity—when all children had was family, friends, and a few simple toys.

I've always loved reading Longfellow, who spent his childhood in then rural Portland, Maine. On that rugged coast he would lean against a great rock and experience the timeless romance of sea and sand. In Deering Woods, he'd climb his favorite tree, where high up, he would find his personal perch, the place where his dreams were born. It was in these quiet places that his future was conceptualized for the first time.

Attempting to recapture those long ago days, many years later, in "My Lost Youth," he wrote:

> I can see the breezy dome of groves,
> The shadows of Deering's Woods;
> And the friendships old and the early loves,
> Come back with a Sabbath sound, as of doves
> In quiet neighborhoods.
> And the verse of that sweet old song,
> It flutters and murmurs still:
> "A boy's will is the wind's will,
> And the thoughts of youth are long, long thoughts."

The Creator, in His great wisdom, gifted each of us with the "long, long thoughts of youth." In this island in time, free from the hurricanes of adult life, the child is to dream and become. Recent studies reveal that the imagination of a child is born in reading and being read to, both creative processes. We must establish a potent counterforce to the millions of media messages our children are bombarded with.

One such counterforce can be found in Christmas stories written by men and women who understand the true meaning of Christmas. The magic of a well-told story is as irresistible as the magic of Christmas itself. Collections of stories, such as these, when internalized over time, can provide the strength to withstand anything society unleashes on our children.

Thus the answer lies, at least in part, in that refuge provided every year by parents—the reading of the stories of Christmas. You will undoubtedly celebrate this season in many ways; let this be one of them. It's a magic ticket for you to once again enter the child's world and for the child to enter a world that can educate and inspire. So, gather your children or grandchildren, make some hot chocolate, and watch their eyes light up as you celebrate this season with them. ✦

The Candle in the Forest

TEMPLE BAILEY

Oh, who could be unhappy at Christmas with a mommy and daddy who loved each other, Pussy-purr-up, Hickory-Dickory-Dock, and onions that would be silver? But was there to be no happiness for the boy-next-door?

"The Candle in the Forest" is an old story that had almost been forgotten. But here and there were those who, having once heard it, were incapable of forgetting it, for it had warmed their hearts all through the years. It reminds us that wealth may be measured in many ways; so can poverty. Often, either is merely a matter of perspective. What a joy it is to bring back from the edge of extinction such a wondrous story!

Temple Bailey, who was born in 1869 and died in 1953, was one of America's most popular (and highest paid) writers early in this century. Both her stories and books had a huge readership. Little is known of her private life—including the exact date of her birth—and her writing reflects both her Christian perspective and her innate idealism. Why do children love the stories of Temple Bailey so much? Perhaps because it's so easy to love the boys and girls in her stories, because the lines have a rhythm to them, and because they're so wonderful to hear read out loud.

The small girl's mother was saying, "The onions will be silver, and the carrots will be gold—"

"And the potatoes will be ivory," said the small girl, and they laughed together. The small girl's mother had a big white bowl in her lap, and she was cutting up vegetables. The onions were the hardest, because she cried over them.

"But our tears will be pearls," said the small girl's mother, and they laughed at that and dried their eyes, and found the carrots much easier, and the potatoes the easiest of all.

Then the next-door-neighbor came in and said, "What are you doing?"

"We are making a vegetable pie for our Christmas dinner," said the small girl's mother.

"And the onions are silver, and the carrots are gold, and the potatoes are ivory," said the small girl.

"I am sure I don't know what you are talking about," said the next-door-neighbor. "We are going to have turkey for dinner, and cranberries and celery."

The small girl laughed and clapped her hands. "But we are going to have a Christmas pie—and the onions will be silver and the carrots gold—"

"You said that once," said the next-door-neighbor, "and I should think you'd know they weren't anything of the kind."

"But they are," said the small girl, all shining eyes and rosy cheeks.

"Run along, darling," said the small girl's mother, "and find poor Pussy-purr-up. He's out in the cold. And you can put on your red sweater and red cap."

So the small girl hopped away like a happy robin, and the next-door-neighbor said, "She's old enough to know that onions aren't silver."

"But they are," said the small girl's mother. "And carrots are gold and the potatoes are—"

The next-door-neighbor's face was flaming. "If you say that again, I'll scream. It sounds silly to me."

"But it isn't in the least silly," said the small girl's mother, and her eyes were blue as sapphires, and as clear as the sea. "It is sensible. When people are poor, they have to make the most of little things. And we'll have only inexpensive things in our pie, but the onions will be silver—"

The lips of the next-door-neighbor were folded in a thin line. "If you had acted like a sensible creature, I shouldn't have asked you for the rent."

The small girl's mother was silent for a moment; then she said, "I am sorry—it ought to be sensible to make the best of things."

"Well," said the next-door-neighbor, sitting down in a chair with a very stiff back, "a pie is a pie. And I wouldn't teach a child to call it anything else."

"I haven't taught her to call it anything else. I was only trying to make her feel that it was something fine and splendid for Christmas Day, so I said that the onions were silver—"

"Don't say that again," snapped the next-door-neighbor, "and I want the rent as soon as possible."

With that, she flung up her head and marched out of the front door, and it slammed behind her and made wild echoes in the little home.

And the small girl's mother stood there alone in the middle of the floor, and her eyes were like the sea in a storm.

But presently the door opened, and the small girl, looking like a red-breast robin, hopped in, and after her came a great black cat with his tail in the air, and he said, "Purr-up," which gave him his name.

And the small girl said, out of the things she had been thinking, "Mother, why don't we have turkey?"

The clear look came back into the eyes of the small girl's mother, and she said, "Because we are content."

And the small girl said, "What is 'content'?"

And her mother said, "It is making the best of what God gives us. And our best for Christmas Day, my darling, is our Christmas pie."

So she kissed the small girl, and they finished peeling the vegetables, and then they put them to simmer on the back of the stove.

After that, the small girl had her supper of bread and milk, and Pussy-purr-up had milk in a saucer on the hearth, and the small girl climbed up in her mother's lap and said, "Tell me a story."

But the small girl's mother said, "Won't it be nicer to talk about Christmas presents?"

And the small girl sat up and said, "Let's."

And the mother said, "Let's tell each other what we'd rather have in the whole wide world."

"Oh, let's," said the small girl. "And I'll tell you first that I want a doll—and I want it to have a pink dress—and I want it to have eyes that open and shut—and I want it to have shoes and stockings—and I want it to have curly hair—" She had to stop, because she didn't have any breath left in her body, and when she got her breath back, she said, "Now, what do you want, Mother, more than anything else in the whole wide world?"

"Well," said the mother, "I want a chocolate mouse."

"Oh," said the small girl scornfully, "I shouldn't think you'd want that."

"Why not?"

"Because a chocolate mouse isn't anything."

"Oh, yes, it is," said the small girl's mother. "A chocolate mouse is Dickory-Dock, and Pussy-Cat-Pussy-Cat-where-have-you-been-was-frightened-under-a-chair, and the mice in Three-Blind-Mice ran after the farmer's wife, and the mouse in A-Frog-Would-a-Wooing-Go went down the throat of the crow—"

And the small girl said, "Could a chocolate mouse do all that?"

"Well," said the small girl's mother, "we could put him on the clock, and under a chair, and cut his tail with a carving knife, and at the very last we could eat him like a crow—"

The small girl said, shivering deliciously, "And he wouldn't be a real mouse?"

"No, just a chocolate one, with cream inside."

"Do you think I'll get one for Christmas?"

"I'm not sure," said the mother.

"Would he be nicer than a doll?"

The small girl's mother hesitated, then told her the truth. "My darling, Mother saved up money for a doll, but the next-door-neighbor wants the rent."

"Hasn't Daddy any more money?"

"Poor Daddy had been sick so long."

"But he's well now."

"I know. But he has to pay for the doctors, and money for medicine, and money for your red sweater, and money for milk for Pussy-purr-up, and money for our pie."

"The boy-next-door says we're poor, Mother."

"We are rich, my darling. We have love, each other, and Pussy-purr-up—"

"His mother won't let him have a cat," said the small girl, with her mind still on the boy-next-door. "But he's going to have a radio."

"Would you rather have a radio than Pussy-purr-up?"

The small girl gave a crow of derision. "I'd rather have Pussy-purr-up than anything else in the whole wide world."

At that, the great cat, who had been sitting on the hearth with his paws tucked under him and his eyes like moons, stretched out his satin-shining length and jumped up on the arm of the chair beside the small girl and her mother, and began to sing a song that was like a mill-wheel away off. He purred to them so loud and so long that at last the small girl grew drowsy.

"Tell me some more about the chocolate mouse," she said, and nodded, and slept.

The small girl's mother carried her into another room, put her to bed, and came back to the kitchen, and it was full of shadows.

But she did not let herself sit among them. She wrapped herself in a great cape and went out into the cold dusk. There was a sweep of wind, heavy clouds overhead, and a band of dull orange showing back of the trees, where the sun had burned down.

She went straight from her little house to the big house of the next-door-neighbor and rang the bell at the back entrance. A maid let her into the kitchen, and there was the next-door-neighbor, and the two women who worked for her, and a daughter-in-law who had come to spend Christmas. The great range was glowing, and things were simmering, and things were stewing, and things were steaming, and things were baking, and things were boiling, and things were broiling, and there were the fragrances of a thousand delicious dishes in the air.

And the next-door-neighbor said, "We are trying to get as much done as possible tonight. We have plans for twelve people for Christmas dinner tomorrow."

And the daughter-in-law, who was all dressed up and had an apron tied about her, said in a sharp voice, "I can't see why you don't let your maids work for you."

And the next-door-neighbor said, "I have always worked. There is no excuse for laziness."

And the daughter-in-law said, "I'm not lazy, if that's what you mean. And we'll never have any dinner if I have to cook it." And away she went out of the kitchen with tears of rage in her eyes.

And the next-door-neighbor said, "If she hadn't gone when she did, I should have told her to go," and there was rage in her eyes but no tears.

She took her hands out of the pan of breadcrumbs and sage, which was being mixed for the stuffing, and said to the small girl's mother, "Did you come to pay the rent?"

The small girl's mother handed her the money, and the next-door-neighbor went upstairs to write a receipt. Nobody asked the small girl's mother to sit down, so she stood in the middle of the floor and sniffed the entrancing fragrances, and looked at the mountain of food which would have served her small family for a month.

While she waited, the boy-next-door came in and said, "Are you the small girl's mother?"

"Yes."

"Are you going to have a tree?"

"Yes."

"Do you want to see mine?"

"It would be wonderful."

So he led her down a long passage to a great room, and there was a tree which touched the ceiling, and on the very top branches and on all the other branches were myriads of little lights which shone like stars, and there were gold bells and silver ones, and red and blue and green balls, and under the tree and on it were toys for boys and toys for girls, and one of the toys was a doll in a pink dress! At that, the heart of the small girl's mother tightened, and she was glad she wasn't a thief, or she would have snatched at the pink doll when the boy wasn't looking, and hidden it under her cape, and run away with it.

The next-door-neighbor-boy was saying, "It's the finest tree anybody has around here. But Dad and Mother don't know that I've seen it."

"Oh, don't they?" said the small girl's mother.

"No," said the boy-next-door, with a wide grin, "and it's fun to fool 'em."

"Is it?" said the small girl's mother. "Now, do

you know, I should think the very nicest thing in the whole world would be not to have seen the tree.

"Because," said the small girl's mother, "the nicest thing in the world would be to have somebody tie a handkerchief around your eyes, so tight, and then to have somebody take your hand and lead you in and out, and in and out, and in and out, until you didn't know where you were, and then to have them untie the handkerchief—and there would be the tree, all shining and splendid!" She stopped, but her singing voice seemed to echo and re-echo in the great room.

The boy's staring eyes had a new look in them. "Did anybody ever tie a handkerchief over your eyes?"

"Oh, yes—"

"And lead you in and out, and in and out?"

"Yes."

"Well, nobody does things like that in our house. They think it's silly."

The small girl's mother laughed, and her laugh tinkled like a bell. "Do you think it's silly?"

He was eager. "No, I don't."

She held out her hand to him. "Will you come and see our tree?"

"Tonight?"

"No, tomorrow morning—early."

"Before breakfast?"

She nodded.

"I'd like it!"

So that was a bargain, and with a quick squeeze of their hands on it. And the small girl's mother went back to the kitchen, and the next-door-neighbor came down with the receipt, and the small girl's mother went out of the back door and found that the orange band which had burned on the horizon was gone, and that there was just the wind and the singing of the trees.

Two men passed her on the brick walk which led to the house, and one of the men was saying, "If you'd only be fair to me, Father."

And the other man said, "All you want of me is money."

"You taught me that, Father."

"Blame it on me—"

"You are to blame. You and mother—did you ever show me the finer things?"

Their angry voices seemed to beat against the noise of the wind and the singing trees, so that the small girl's mother shivered, and drew her cape around her, and ran as fast as she could to her little house.

There were all the shadows to meet her, but she did not sit among them. She made coffee and a dish of milk toast, and set the toast in the oven to keep hot, and then she stood at the window watching. At last she saw through the darkness what looked like a star low down, and she knew that that star was a lantern, and she ran and opened the door wide.

And her young husband set the lantern down on the threshold, and took her in his arms, and said, "The sight of you is more than food and drink."

When he said that, she knew he had had a hard day, but her heart leaped because she knew that what he had said of her was true.

Then they went into the house together, and she set the food before him. And that he might forget his hard day, she told him of her own. And when she came to the part about the next-door-neighbor and the rent, she said, "I am telling you this because it has a happy ending."

And he put his hands over hers and said, "Everything with you has a happy ending."

"Well, this is a happy ending," said the small girl's mother, with all the sapphires in her eyes emphasizing it. "Because when I went over to pay the rent, I was feeling how poor we were and wishing that I had a pink doll for Baby, and books for you, and, and—and a magic carpet to carry us away from work and worry. And then I went into the parlor and saw the tree—with everything hanging on it that was glittering and gorgeous, and then I came home." Her breath was quick and her lips smiling. "I came home—and I was glad I lived in my little home."

"What made you glad, dearest?"

"Oh, love is here; and hate is there, and a boy's deceit, and a man's injustice. They were saying sharp things to each other—and—and—their dinner will be a stalled ox—and in my little house is the faith of a child in the goodness of God, and the bravery of a man who fought for his country—"

She was in his arms now.

"And the blessing of a woman who has never known defeat." His voice broke on the words.

In that moment it seemed as if the wind stopped blowing, and as if the trees stopped sighing, as if there was the sound of heavenly singing.

The small girl's mother and the small girl's father sat up very late that night. They popped a great bowlful of crisp snowy corn and made it into balls; they boiled sugar and molasses, and cracked nuts, and made candy of them. They cut funny little Christmas fairies out of paper and painted their jackets bright red, with round silver buttons of the tinfoil that came on cream cheese. And then they put the balls and the candy and the painted fairies and a long red candle in a big basket, and set it away. And the small girl's mother brought out the chocolate mouse.

"We will put this on the clock," she said, "where her eyes will rest on it first thing in the morning."

So they put it there, and it seemed as natural as life, so that Pussy-purr-up positively licked his chops and sat in front of the clock as if to keep

his eye on the chocolate mouse. The small girl's mother said, "She was lovely about giving up the doll, and she will love the tree."

"We'll have to get up very early," said the small girl's father.

"And you'll have to run ahead to light the candle."

Well, they got up before dawn the next morning, and so did the boy-next-door. He was there on the step, waiting, blowing on his hands and beating them quite like the poor little boys do in a Christmas story, who haven't any mittens. But he wasn't a poor little boy, and he had so many pairs of fur-trimmed gloves that he didn't know what to do with them, but he had left the house in such a hurry that he had forgotten to put them on. So there he stood on the front step of the little house, blowing on his hands and beating them. And it was dark, with a sort of pale shine in the heavens, which didn't seem to come from the stars or the herald of the dawn; it was just a mystical silver glow that set the boy's heart to beating.

He had never been out alone like this. He had always stayed in his warm bed until somebody called him, and then he had waited until they had called again, and then he had dressed and gone to breakfast, where his father scolded because he was late, and his mother scolded because he ate too fast. But this day had begun with adventure, and for the first time, under that silvery sky, he felt the thrill of it.

Then suddenly someone came around the house—someone tall and thin, with a cap on his head and an empty basket in his hands.

"Hello," he said. "A merry Christmas!"

It was the small girl's father, and he put the key in the lock and went in, and turned on a light, and there was the table set for four.

And the small girl's father said, "You see we have set a place for you. We must eat something before we go out."

And the boy said, "Are we going out? I came to see the tree."

"We are going out to see the tree."

Before the boy could ask any questions, the small girl's mother appeared with fingers on her lips and said, "Sh-sh," and then she began to recite in a hushed voice, "Hickory-Dickory-Dock—"

Then there was a little cry and the sound of dancing feet, and the small girl in a red dressing gown came flying in.

"Oh, Mother, Mother, the mouse is on the clock—the mouse is on the clock!"

Well, it seemed to the little boy that he had never seen anything so exciting as the things that followed. The chocolate mouse went up the clock and under the chair and would have had its tail

cut off except that the small girl begged to save it.

"I want to keep it as it is, Mother."

And playing this game as if it were the most important thing in the whole wide world were the small girl's mother and the small girl's father, all laughing and flushed, and chanting the quaint old words to the quaint old music. The boy-next-door held his breath for fear he would wake up from this entrancing dream and find himself in his own big house, alone in his puffy bed, or eating breakfast with his stodgy parents who had never played with him in his life. He found himself laughing too, and flushed and happy, and trying to sing in his funny boy's voice.

The small girl absolutely refused to eat the mouse. "He's my darling Christmas mouse, Mother."

So her mother said, "Well, I'll put him on the clock again, where Pussy-purr-up can't get him while we are out."

"Oh, are we going out?" said the small girl, round-eyed.

"Yes."

"Where are we going?"

"To find Christmas."

That was all the small girl's mother would tell. So they had breakfast, and everything tasted perfectly delicious to the boy-next-door. But

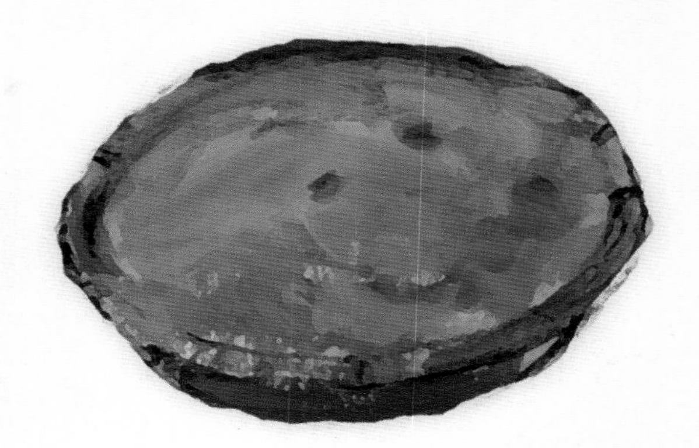

first they bowed their heads, and the small girl's father said, "Dear Christ-Child, on this Christmas morning, bless these children, and keep our hearts young and full of love for Thee."

The boy-next-door, when he lifted his head, had a funny feeling as if he wanted to cry, and yet it was a lovely feeling, all warm and comfortable inside.

For breakfast they each had a great baked apple, and great slices of sweet bread and butter, and great glasses of milk, and as soon as they had finished, away they went out of the door and down into the woods in back of the house, and when they were deep into the woods, the small girl's father took out of his pocket a little flute and began to play; he played thin piping tunes that went flitting around among the trees, and the small girl and her mother hummed the tunes until it sounded like singing bees, and their

feet fairly danced and the boy found himself humming and dancing with them.

Then suddenly the piping ceased, and a hush fell over the woods. It was so still that they could almost hear each other breathe—so still that when a light flamed suddenly in that open space, it burned without a flicker.

The light came from a red candle that was set in the top of a small living tree. It was the only light on the tree, but it showed the snowy balls, and the small red fairies whose coats had silver buttons.

"It's our tree, my darling," he heard the small girl's mother saying.

Suddenly it seemed to the boy that his heart would burst in his breast. He wanted someone to speak to him like that. The small girl sat high on her father's shoulders, and her father held her mother's hand. It was like a chain of gold, their holding hands like that, the loving each other.

The boy reached out and touched the woman's hand. She looked down at him and drew him close. He felt warmed and comforted. Their candle burning there in the darkness was like some sacred fire of friendship. He wished that it would never go out, that he might stand there watching it, with his small cold hand in the clasp of the small girl's mother's hand.

It was late when the boy-next-door got back to his own big house. But he had not been missed. Everybody was up, and everything was upset. The daughter-in-law had declared the night before that she would not stay another day beneath that roof, and off she had gone with her young husband, and her little girl, who was to have the pink doll on the tree.

"And good riddance," said the next-door-neighbor. But she ate no breakfast, and she went to the kitchen and worked with her maids to get the dinner ready, and there were covers laid for nine instead of twelve.

And the next-door-neighbor kept saying, "Good riddance—good riddance," and not once did she say, "A merry Christmas."

But the boy-next-door had something in his heart that was warm and glowing like the candle in the forest, and he came to his mother and said, "May I have the pink dolly?"

She spoke frowningly. "What does a boy want of a doll?"

"I'd like to give it to the little girl next door."

"Do you think I can buy dolls to give away in charity?"

"Well, they gave me a Christmas present."

"What did they give you?"

He opened his hand and showed a little flute tied with a gay red ribbon. He lifted it to his lips and blew on it, a thin piping tune.

"Oh, that," said his mother scornfully. "Why, that's nothing but a reed from the pond."

But the boy knew it was more than that. It was a magic pipe that made you dance, and made your heart warm and happy.

So he said again, "I'd like to give her the doll." And he reached out his little hand and touched his mother's—and his eyes were wistful.

His mother's own eyes softened—she had lost one son that day—and she said, "Oh, well, do as you please," and went back to the kitchen.

The boy-next-door ran into the great room and took the doll from the tree, and wrapped her in paper, and flew out of the door and down the brick walk and straight into the little house. When the door was opened, he saw that his friends were just sitting down to dinner—and there was the pie, all brown and piping hot, with a wreath of holly, and the small girl was saying, "And the onions were silver, and the carrots were gold—"

The boy-next-door went up to the small girl and said, "I've brought you a present."

With his eyes all lighted up, he took off the paper in which it was wrapped, and there was the doll, in rosy frills, with eyes that opened and shut, and shoes and stockings, and curly hair that was bobbed and beautiful.

And the small girl, in a whirlwind of happiness, said, "Is it really my doll?" And the boy-next-door felt very shy and happy, and he said, "Yes."

And the small girl's mother said, "It was a beautiful thing to do," and she bent and kissed him. Again that bursting feeling came into the boy's heart and he lifted his face to hers and said, "May I come sometimes and be your boy?"

And she said, "Yes."

And when at last he went away, she stood in the door and watched him, such a little lad, who knew so little of loving. And because she knew so much of love, her eyes filled to overflowing.

But presently she wiped the tears away and went back to the table; and she smiled at the small girl and at the small girl's father.

"And the potatoes were ivory," she said. "Oh, who would ask for turkey, when they can have pie like this?" ✦

Christmas Memories

Favorite Family Recipes

Favorite Family Decorations

The Last Straw

PAULA MCDONALD

"But what if I pick someone's name that I don't like?" asked Kelly.

One of the most beautiful Christmas stories of the 1970's was written about a quarreling family and what one mother did to restore a sense of caring to their familial relationships. I personally feel that this particular story will wear very well down through the years and will be with us for a long time to come.

The story was viewed as so special to the editors of David C. Cook/Chariot that they printed it as a separate book (featuring a cardboard pull-out cradle) in the fall of 1992.

To truly share this season of love and laughter, even a little boy must first discover Christmas in his heart.

Paula McDonald, winner of a number of prestigious writing awards, today lives in Baja, California. In recent years, she has become a mainstay of the *Reader's Digest* stable of writers.

Everyone, unfortunately, was cooped up in the house that typical gray winter afternoon. And, as usual, the four little McNeals were at it again, teasing each other, squabbling, bickering, always fighting over their toys.

At times like this, Ellen was almost ready to believe that her children didn't love each other, even though she knew that wasn't true. All brothers and sisters fight sometimes, of course, but lately her lively little bunch had been particularly horrid to each other, especially Eric and Kelly, who were only a year apart. The two of them seemed determined to spend the whole long winter making each other miserable.

"Give me that. It's mine!" Kelly screamed, her voice shrill.

"It is not! I had it first," Eric answered stubbornly.

Ellen sighed as she listened to the latest argument. With Christmas only a month away, the house seemed sadly lacking in Christmas spirit.

This was supposed to be the season of sharing and love, of warm feelings and happy hearts. A home needed more than just pretty packages and twinkling lights on a tree to fill the holidays with joy.

Ellen had only one idea. Years ago, her grandmother had told her about an old custom that helped people discover the true meaning of Christmas. Perhaps it would work for her family this year. It was certainly worth a try.

She gathered the children together and lined them up on the couch, tallest to smallest—Eric, Kelly, Lisa and Mike.

"How would you kids like to start a new Christmas tradition this year?" she asked. "It's like a game, but it can only be played by people who can keep a secret. Can everyone here do that?"

"I can!" shouted Eric.

"I can keep a secret better than him!" yelled Kelly.

"I can do it!" chimed in Lisa.

"Me too. Me too," squealed little Mike. "I'm big enough."

"Well then, this is how the game works," Ellen explained. "This year we're going to surprise Baby Jesus when He comes on Christmas Eve by making Him the softest bed in the world. We're going to fill a little crib with straw to make it comfortable. But here's the secret part. The straw we put in will measure the good deeds we've done, but we won't tell anyone who we're doing them for."

The children looked confused. "But how will Jesus know it's His bed?" Kelly asked.

"He'll know," said Ellen. "He'll recognize it by the love we put in to make it soft."

"But who will we do the good deeds for?" asked Eric, still a little confused.

"We'll do them for each other. Once a week we'll put all of our names in a hat, mine and Daddy's too. Then we'll each pick out a different name. Whoever's name we draw, we'll do kind things for that person for a whole week. But you can't tell anyone else whose name you've chosen. We'll each try to do as many favors for our special person as we can without getting caught. And for every good deed we do, we'll put another straw in the crib."

"Like being a spy!" squealed Lisa.

"But what if I pick someone's name that I don't like?" Kelly frowned.

Ellen thought about that for a minute. "Maybe you could use an extra fat piece of straw. And think how much faster the fat straws will fill up our crib. We'll use the cradle in the attic," she said. "And we can all go to the field behind the school for the straw."

Without a single argument, the children bundled into their wool hats and mittens, laughing and tumbling out of the house. The field had been covered with tall grass in summer, but now, dead and dried, the golden stalks looked just like real straw. They carefully selected handfuls and placed them in the large box they had carried with them.

"That's enough," Ellen laughed when the box was almost overflowing. "Remember, it's only a small cradle."

So home they went to spread their straw carefully on a large tray Ellen never used. Eric, because he was the eldest, was given the responsibility of climbing into the attic and bringing down the cradle.

"We'll pick names as soon as Daddy comes home for dinner," Ellen said, unable to hide a smile at the thought of Mark's pleased reaction to the children's transformed faces and their voices, filled now with excited anticipation rather than annoyance.

At the supper table that night, six pieces of paper were folded, shuffled and shaken around in Mark's furry winter hat, and the drawing began. Kelly picked a name first and immediately started to giggle. Lisa reached into the hat next, trying hard to look like a serious spy. Mike couldn't read yet, so Mark whispered the name in his ear. Then Mike quickly ate his little wad of paper so no one would ever learn the identity of his secret person. Eric was the next person to choose, and as he unfolded his scrap of paper, a frown creased his forehead. But he stuffed the name quickly into his pocket and said nothing. Ellen and Mark selected names and the family was ready to begin.

The week that followed was filled with surprises, it seemed the McNeal house had suddenly been invaded by an army of invisible elves. Kelly would walk into her room at bedtime to find her nightgown neatly laid out and her bed

turned down. Someone cleaned up the sawdust under the workbench without being asked. The jelly blobs magically disappeared from the kitchen counter after lunch one day while Ellen was out getting the mail. And every morning, when Eric was brushing his teeth, someone crept quietly into his room and made the bed. It wasn't made perfectly, but it was made. That particular little elf must have had short arms because he couldn't seem to reach the middle.

"Where are my shoes?" Mark asked one morning. No one seemed to know, but suddenly, before he left for work, they were back in the closet again, freshly shined.

Ellen noticed other changes during that week too. The children weren't teasing or fighting as much. An argument would start, and then suddenly stop right in the middle for no apparent reason. Even Eric and Kelly seemed to be getting along better and bickering less. In fact, there were times when all the children could be seen smiling secret smiles and giggling to themselves. And slowly, one by one, the first straws began to appear in the little crib. Just a few, then a few more each day. By the end of the first week, a little pile had accumulated.

Everyone was anxious to pick new names, and this time there was more laughter and merriment than there had been the first time. Except for Eric. Once again, he unfolded his scrap of paper, glanced at it, and stuffed it in his pocket without a word.

The second week brought more astonishing events, and the little pile of straw in the manger grew higher and softer. There was more laughter, less teasing, and hardly any arguments could be heard around the house. Only Eric had been unusually quiet, and sometimes Ellen would catch him looking a little sad. But the straws in the manger continued to pile up.

At last, it was almost Christmas. They chose names for the final time on the night before Christmas Eve. As they sat around the table waiting for the last set of names to be shaken in the hat, the children smiled as they looked at their hefty pile of straws. They all knew it was comfortable and soft, but there was one day left and they could still make it a little deeper, a little softer, and they were going to try.

For the last time the hat was passed around the table. Mike picked out a name, and again quickly ate the paper as he had done each week. Lisa unfolded hers carefully under the table, peeked at it and then hunched up her little shoulders, smiling. Kelly reached into the hat and grinned from ear to ear when she saw the name. Ellen and Mark each took their turn and handed the hat with the last name to Eric. As he unfolded the scrap of paper and glanced at it, his face crumpled and he seemed about to cry. Without a word, he turned and ran from the room.

Everyone immediately jumped up from the table, but Ellen stopped them. "No! Stay where you are," she said firmly. "I'll go."

In his room, Eric was trying to pull on his coat with one hand while he picked up a small cardboard suitcase with the other.

"I have to leave," he said quietly through his tears. "If I don't, I'll spoil Christmas."

"But why? And where are you going?"

"I can sleep in my snow fort for a couple of days. I'll come home right after Christmas, I promise."

Ellen started to say something about freezing and snow and no mittens or boots, but Mark, who had come up behind her, gently laid his hand on her arm and shook his head. The front door closed, and together they watched from the window as the little figure with the sadly slumped shoulders trudged across the street and sat down on a snowbank near the corner. It was dark outside, and cold, and a few flurries drifted down on the small boy and his suitcase.

"Give him a few minutes alone," said Mark quietly. "I think he needs that. Then you can talk to him."

The huddled figure was already dusted with white when Ellen walked across the street and sat down beside him on the snowbank.

"What is it, Eric? You've been so good these last few weeks, but I know something's been bothering you since we first started the crib. Can you tell me, honey?"

"Ah, Mom . . . don't you see?" He sniffed. "I tried so hard, but I can't do it anymore, and now I'm going to wreck Christmas for everybody." With that, he burst into sobs and threw himself into his mother's arms.

"Mom." The little boy choked. "You just don't know. I got Kelly's name every time! And I hate Kelly! I tried, Mom. I really did. I snuck in her room every night and fixed her bed. I even laid out her crummy nightgown. I let her use my race car one day, but she smashed it right into the wall, like always! Every week, when we picked new names, I thought it would be over. Tonight, when I got her name again, I knew I couldn't do it anymore. If I try, I'll probably punch her instead. If I stay home and beat Kelly up, I'll spoil Christmas for everybody."

The two of them sat there together quietly for a few minutes and then Ellen spoke softly. "Eric, I'm so proud of you. Every good deed you did should count double because it was hard for you to be nice to Kelly for so long. But you did those good deeds anyway, one straw at a time. You gave your love when it wasn't easy to give. And maybe that's what the spirit of Christmas is really all about. And maybe it's the hard good deeds and the difficult straws that make that little crib special. You're the one who's probably added the most important straws this year." Ellen paused, stroking the head pressed tightly against her shoulder. "Now, how would you like a chance to earn a few easy straws like the rest of us? I still have the name I picked in my pocket, and I haven't looked at it yet. Why don't we switch, for the last day? And it will be our secret."

Eric lifted his head and looked into her face, his eyes wide. "That's not cheating?"

"It's not cheating." And together they dried the tears, brushed off the snow, and walked back to the house.

The next day, the whole family was busy cooking and straightening up the house for Christmas Day, wrapping last-minute presents and trying hard to keep from bursting with excitement. But even with all the activity and eagerness, a flurry of new straws piled up in the crib, and by nightfall the little manger was almost overflowing. At different times while passing by, each member of the family, big and small, would pause and look at the wondrous pile for a moment, then smile before going on. But . . . who could really know? One more straw still might make a difference.

For that reason, just before bedtime, Ellen tiptoed quietly to Kelly's room to lay out the little blue nightgown and turn down the bed. But she stopped in the doorway, surprised. Someone had already been there. The nightgown was laid across the bed, and a small red race car had been placed next to it on the pillow.

The last straw was Eric's after all. ✦

A beautiful new treatment of this story is being published fall of 2007 by Covenant Communications, Inc.

Christmas Memories

Christmas Eve Memories

Christmas Day Memories

Other Special Holiday Events

The Tallest Angel

AUTHOR UNKNOWN

"Do you think I could look like a tall angel? I'm smaller than anyone else because my back is so bent. Do you think I could look like a tall angel?"

Some stories are like a well-loved and mauled teddy bear—they are able to become far more valuable after living with them than they were brand-new. This is such a story. It has warmed my heart—and scolded me—ever since I first heard it many years ago. It is one of those stories that sneaks up on a person, and then, as it sits in your head, you begin to understand the deep meaning it holds. It explores a subject many of us avoid: how we treat the unlovely among us. Let's face it—it's as hard not to care for the beautiful ones as it is to care for the unattractive and unresponsive. Just as we could profit with reading I Corinthians 13 every day of our lives, so could we from this story. Were we to do so, ours would be a more caring world. I've never been able to find out who wrote this story. But one thing I do know, it had to be a very special person to be able to teach us this very important lesson in love.

od doesn't love me!" The words echoed sharply through the thoughts of Miss Ellis as she looked around the fourth-grade school room. Her gaze skipped lightly over the many bent heads and then rested on one in particular. "God doesn't love me!" The words had struck her mind so painfully that her mouth opened slightly in mute protest.

The child under Miss Ellis's troubled study lifted her head for a moment, scanned her classmates briefly, then bent to her book again.

Ever since the first day of school, Miss Ellis had been hurt and troubled by those bitter assertions. "God doesn't love me!" The words had come from the small nine-year-old girl that stirred again restively under the continued scrutiny of Miss Ellis. Then, bending her head to her own desk, Miss Ellis prayed in her heart for the nth time: "Help her, dear

God, and help me to help her. Please show Dory that you do love her too."

Dory sat with her geography book open upon her desk, but the thoughts that raced through her mind were not concerned with the capital of Ohio. A moment before she had felt the warm eyes of Miss Ellis upon her, and now angry sentences played tag with each other in her bowed head. Once again she heard the calm voice of Miss Ellis.

"God wants us to be happy in His love"—Dory laughed bitterly to herself. How could anyone be happy with a hunched back and leg braces!

"God loves everyone," Miss Ellis had said, to which Dory had angrily replied, "But he doesn't love me—that's why He made me ugly and crippled."

"God is good."

"God is not good to me. He's mean to me! That's what—to let me grow so crooked."

Dory raised her head and looked at the children around her. Mary Ann had long golden curls; Dory had straight brown hair, pulled back tight and braided into an unlovely pigtail. Jeanetta had china blue eyes that twinkled like evening stars; Dory had brown eyes that seemed smoky, so full of bitterness were they. Ellen Sue had a pink rosebud mouth that readily spread into a happy smile. Well, Ellen Sue could smile. She had a lovely dimpled body and ruffled, ribboned dresses. But why should Dory smile? Her mouth was straight and tight, and her body hunched and twisted. Anyone would laugh to see ruffles on her dresses. No pink and blue dresses for her, only straight dark gowns that hung like sacks over her small hunched frame.

Suddenly hate and anger so filled the heart of the little girl that she felt she must get away from this roomful of straight-bodied children or choke. She signaled her desire to Miss Ellis, who nodded permission.

There was neither pity nor laughter in the eyes that followed Dory to the door, only casual indifference. The children had long since accepted Dory as she was. No one ever jeered at her awkwardness, nor did anyone fuss over her in pity. The children did not mean to be unkind, but knowing the limits of Dory's mobility, they usually ran off to their active games, leaving her a lonely little spectator.

Miss Ellis saw the children settle back to their studies as the door closed after Dory. She stared at

the door, not seeing the door at all, only the small, hunchbacked girl.

"What can I do to help her to be happy?" she pondered. "What can anyone say or do to comfort and encourage such a child?"

She had talked to Dory's parents and had found them to be of little help. They seemed inclined to feel that Dory's crippled condition was a blot upon them, one which they did not deserve. Miss Ellis had urged them not to try to explain Dory's condition but to accept it as God's will and try to seek His blessings through acceptance of His will. They were almost scornful to the idea that any blessing could be found in a crippled, unhappy child, but they did agree to come to church and to bring Dory as often as possible.

"Please help Dory," prayed Miss Ellis. "Help Dory and her parents too." Then the hall bell sounded, and Miss Ellis arose to dismiss her class.

The reds, yellows and greens of autumn faded into the white of winter. The Christmas season was unfolding in the room. Tiny Christmas trees stood shyly on the window sills. A great green wreath covered the door. Its silver bells jingled whenever the door moved, and the delighted giggles of the children echoed in return. The blue-white shadows of a winter afternoon were creeping across the snow as Miss Ellis watched the excited children set up the manger scene on the low sand table.

"Christmas," thought Miss Ellis, "is a time of peace and joy. Even the children feel the spirit and try to be nicer to one another."

"Is your Christmas dress done yet, Ellen Sue?"

Without waiting for an answer, Mary Ann chattered on, "Mother got material for mine today—it's red, real red velvet. Oh, I can hardly wait, can you?"

"Mine is all done but the hem." Ellen Sue fairly trembled with excitement. "It's pink, with rosebuds made of ribbon."

Miss Ellis smiled, remembering the thrill of the Christmas dresses of her own girlhood. How carefully they were planned, and how lovingly her mother had made each one. Miss Ellis leaned back to cherish the memories a moment longer. Then a movement caught her eye. Slowly, furtively, with storm-filled eyes, Dory was backing away from the chattering children. Her heart stirred with sympathy. Miss Ellis watched the unhappy child ease herself into her chair, pull a book from her desk, and bend her head over it. "She isn't studying," thought Miss Ellis. "She is only pretending—to cover up her misery."

Dory stared at the book in front of her, fighting against the tears that demanded release. What if one of the girls had asked her about her Christmas dress? Her Christmas dress indeed! Would anyone call a brown sack of a dress a Christmas dress? Would the children laugh? No, Dory knew the girls wouldn't laugh. They would just feel sorry for her and her shapeless dress. Sometimes that was almost worse than if they would laugh. At least then she would have an excuse to pour out the angry words that crowded into her throat.

"Dory," a warm voice broke in upon her thoughts. "Dory will you help me with these Christmas decorations? You could walk along and hold them for me while I pin them up, please."

Dory arose, thankful for the diversion and thankful to be near Miss Ellis. The silver tinsel was pleasant to hold, and Miss Ellis always made her feel so much better.

Slowly they proceeded around the room, draping the tinsel garland as they went. The babble of voices in the corner by the sand table took on a new note, an insistent clamoring tone that finally burst forth in a rush of small bodies in the direction of Miss Ellis.

"Please, Miss Ellis, can I be Mary in the Christmas program?"

"Miss Ellis, I'd like to be Joseph."

"I should be Mary because I can't sing in the angel choir."

Miss Ellis raised her hand for quiet. After a moment she began, "I've already chosen the ones who will play the parts of Mary, Joseph, the shepherds, and the angel choir."

"Tell us the names; tell us the names now," the children chorused.

"All right," agreed Miss Ellis as she reached for a paper from her desk. "Here they are: Sue Ellen will be Mary; Daniel will be Joseph; John, Allen and Morris will be the shepherds. All the rest of you will be choir angels—"

Miss Ellis scanned the eager hopeful faces around her till she saw the upturned face of Dory. There was no eager hope in her small pinched face. Dory felt from bitter experience that no one wanted a hunchback in a program. Miss Ellis could not bear the numb resignation on that small white face. Almost without realizing what she was saying, she finished the sentence. "All will be choir angels except Dory." There was a moment of hushed surprise. "Dory will be the special angel who talks to the shepherds."

All the children gasped and turned to look at Dory. Dory, a special angel? They had never thought of that. As realization penetrated Dory's amazement, a slow smile relaxed the pinched features, a little candle flame of happiness shone in the brown eyes.

"Her eyes are lovely when she's happy," marveled Miss Ellis. "Oh, help her to be happy more often!"

The hall bell sounded the end of another school day, and soon all the children had bidden Miss Ellis good-bye as they hurried from the room.

All but one. All but Dory. She stood very still, as if clinging to a magic moment for as long as possible. The lights had flickered out of her eyes, and her face seemed whiter than ever before.

Miss Ellis knelt and took Dory's cold little hands in her own. "What is it, Dory? Don't you want to be a special angel after all?"

"I do, I do—" Dory's voice broke. "But—but— I'll be a horrid hunchbacked angel. Everyone will stare at me and laugh because angels are straight and beauti—" Dory's small body shook with uncontrollable sobs.

"Listen to me, Dory," Miss Ellis began slowly. "You are going to be my special angel. Somehow I'm going to make you look straight and beautiful, like real angels. Will you just be happy, Dory, and let me plan it all out? Then I'll tell you all about it."

Dory lifted her head hopefully "Do you think you can, Miss Ellis, do you think you can?"

"I know I can, Dory. Smile now, you're so pretty when you smile. And say over and over, 'God loves me, God loves me.' That will make you want to smile. Will you try it, Dory?"

A shadow of disbelief crossed Dory's face. Then she brightened with resolution.

"I'll say it, Miss Ellis, and if you can make me look like a straight angel, I'll try to believe it."

"That's the spirit, Dory. Good-bye, now, and have nice dreams tonight."

Dory went to the door, paused a moment, then turned again to Miss Ellis.

"Yes, Dory, is there something else?"

Dory hesitated for a long moment. Then she said slowly, "Do you think I could look like a tall angel too? I'm smaller than anyone else because my back is so bent. Do you think I could look like a tall angel?"

"I'm sure we can make you look tall," promised Miss Ellis recklessly.

Dory sighed with satisfaction and let the door swing shut behind her. The silver bells on the Christmas wreath jingled merrily, almost mockingly.

"What have I done?" thought Miss Ellis soberly. "I have promised a little crooked girl that she will be a tall, straight angel. I haven't the slightest idea how I am going to do it. Dear God, please help

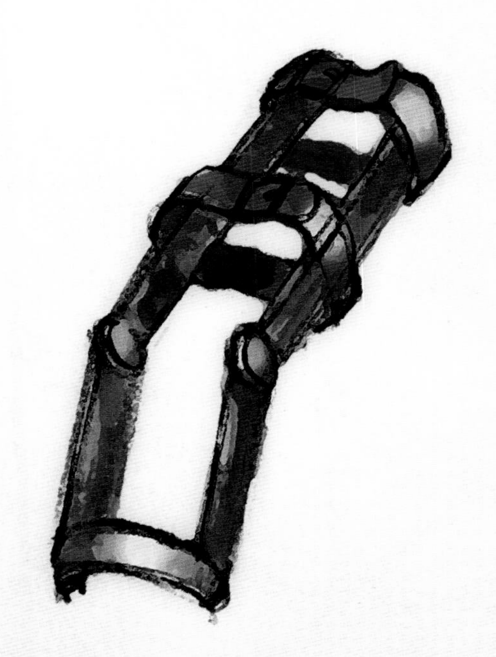

me—show me the way. For the first time since I've known her, I have seen Dory happy. Please help her to be happy in Your love, dear God. Show me the way to help her."

Miss Ellis went to sleep that night with the prayer still in her heart.

Morning came crisp and clear. Lacy frills of frost hung daintily from every branch and bush. Miss Ellis rubbed her eyes and looked out of her window. The sparkling white beauty of the morning reminded her of angels. Angels! She recalled her promise. She had dreamed of angels too. What was the dream about, what was it? Miss Ellis tapped her finger against her lip in concentration. Suddenly, as if a dark door had opened to the sunshine, the dream, the whole angel plan swept into her mind. Idea after idea tumbled about like dancing sunbeams. She must hurry and dress; she must get to the schoolhouse early to talk to Joe, the janitor. Joe could do anything, and she was sure that Joe would help her.

At the door of the school she scarcely paused to stomp the snow from her boots. Quickly she went down to the furnace room where Joe was stoking coal into the hungry furnace.

"Joe," she began. "I need your help. I've got a big job ahead of me. I'm going to make little Dory Saunders into a tall, straight angel for our Christmas pageant."

Joe thumped his shovel down, looked at her intently, and scratched his head. "You certainly did pick yourself a job, Miss Ellis. How you going to do all this, and where do I figure?"

"It's like this, Joe," and she outlined her plan to him, and Joe agreed to it.

Miss Ellis went lightly up the steps to her fourth-grade room. She greeted the children cheerily, smiling warmly at Dory. Dory returned the smile, with the candle flames of happiness glowing again in her eyes.

For Dory the day was enchanted. Round-faced angels smiled at her through the O's in her arithmetic book. The time passed dreamily on whirring angel wings. At last, school was over, and she was alone with Miss Ellis, waiting to hear the marvelous plan that would make her a straight and beautiful angel.

"I've thought it all out, Dory." Miss Ellis pulled Dory close as she explained the plan. "Mrs. Brown and I are going to make you a long white gown and wings, and Joe will fix you up so you will be the tallest angel of all. But, Dory, let's keep it a secret until the night of the program, shall we?"

Dory nodded vigorously. She couldn't speak. The vision was too lovely for words; so she just nodded and hugged Miss Ellis as tight as her thin arms could squeeze. Then she limped from the room.

Dory had never felt such happiness. Now she really had a place in the scheme of events. At

least until Christmas, she felt, she really belonged with the other children. She was really like other children. Maybe God loved even her.

At last, the night of the program came. Carols of praise to the newborn King rang through the school.

Now it was time for the Christmas pageant. Soft music invited a quiet mood, and the audience waited for the curtains to open upon a shepherd scene.

The sky was dark as the shepherds sat huddled around their fire. Then suddenly a bright light burst over the scene. The audience gasped in surprise. High up on a pedestal, dressed in a gown of shimmering white satin, Dory raised her arms in salutation.

"Fear not." Her face was radiant as she spoke. "For, behold, I bring you good tidings of great joy, which shall be to all people." Her voice gathered conviction as she continued, "For unto you is born this day in the city of David a Saviour, which is Christ, the Lord."

The triumphant ring in her voice carried to the choir, and the children sang, "Glory to God in the highest, and on earth peace, good will toward men," as they had never sung before.

Dory's father blinked hard at the tears that stung his eyes, and he thought in his heart, "Why she's a beautiful child. Why doesn't Martha curl her hair and put a ribbon in it?"

Dory's mother closed her eyes on the lovely vision, praying silently, "Forgive me, God; I haven't appreciated the good things about Dory because I've been so busy complaining about her misfortunes."

The sound of the carols sung by the choir died away, and the curtains silently closed.

Miss Ellis hurried backstage and lifted Dory from her high pedestal.

"Dory," she asked softly, "what happened? How did you feel when you were the angel? Something wonderful happened to you. I saw it in your face."

Dory hesitated. "You'll laugh—"

"Never, never, Dory, I promise!"

"Well, while I was saying the angel message, I began to feel taller and taller and real straight." She paused and looked intently at Miss Ellis.

"Go on, dear," urged Miss Ellis gently. "What else?"

"Well, I didn't feel my braces anymore. And do you know what?"

"No, what? Tell me."

"Right then I knew it was true. God does love me."

"Dory, as long as you know that is true, you'll never be really unhappy again. And someday, my dear, you will stand straight and tall and beautiful among the real angels in heaven. ✦

Christmas Memories

Christmas Activities at School

Christmas Activities at Church

The Night My Father Came Home

AUTHOR UNKNOWN

"He promised I'd get some marbles . . . and a baseball glove . . . and a football . . . and an electric train. And then he went away."

A wish list for Santa seldom includes asking for a father, but this time it does. Santa has to play matchmaker to help Joe out on a very big Christmas wish. How I wish I could find out who wrote this funny story, for it is almost impossible to listen to it without laughing. And, it is one of the only Christmas stories I've ever read that sounds like a little boy actually wrote it.

y mother said he was gone for good, but I thought if I wrote to Santa Claus . . .

As soon as I wrote the letter I went down to the post office to mail it, so it would get there in time. Boy, there were about a million people standing in line and everything, and in there was all that Christmas music coming out of a big horn on the wall.

Pretty soon I found the place in the wall where you put letters in, but it was too high up. So I went out again and I went around to the back of the post office, where there were these big doors open and a man was carrying boxes out to a truck. There must have been a million boxes. I never saw so many.

There was nobody there but him. He was kind of tall and thin and his face was dirty from where he kept rubbing his hand across it. He had freckles and his ears stuck out. I don't know how old he was. Pretty old. Twenty-five, I guess, like my father. He kept picking up

these boxes and throwing them on the truck, and he didn't see me, so I yanked on his coat.

"Here's a letter," I said. "The place out there where you're supposed to put it in is too high up."

He was lifting this big box, and he stopped and looked at me. It was kind of a mad look. Then he looked down at the letter and he made a noise like my father the time he never saw this skate I left in the hall until he kind of slid downstairs on it.

"That's what I've been waiting for," he said. "A letter to Santa Claus." He kind of groaned. "It might interest you to know that we have sent out one hundred and forty-three thousand pieces of mail in the past week and that there will be at least twice that much in the next three days before Christmas. This makes my day complete."

I was glad he was glad even if he didn't look so happy. He didn't take the letter, so I held it out again. "Will it get there right away?" I said. "It's important."

"How old are you?" he said. He still sounded mad.

"Six," I said. "Well, five."

"What's your name?" he said.

"Joe," I said.

"Look, Joe," he said. He sure looked like he was going to yell at me, but all of a sudden he didn't, like my father the time I took his shaving soap to make some frosting for my mud pies. "Joe, I can't take your letter," he said. "Believe me. It won't go any place . . . I mean, Santa Claus has already left the North Pole, see, so he can't get any more letters. So just take it back to your folks. They'll take care of it for you."

He didn't understand anything. "Look, I haven't got folks," I said. "I mean, I've got a mother, but she works in a store all day and I have to stay with Mrs. Henderson next door all the time after I get back from school. That's what I wrote in the letter. I want my father to come home."

"Where'd he go?" He looked at me kind of funny, like he was waiting for something. He was sure dumb.

"He just went away," I said. "He just got hurt in an accident and then he went away. My mother said he won't ever come back any more, but I want to surprise her. He's got to come back for Christmas, on account of he promised I would get some marbles and a baseball glove and a football and an electric train. Last year I wasn't old enough, but I am now."

The way he acted, you'd think he didn't hardly even listen to what I said. He didn't even say anything. He just kept on looking at me, and after awhile he kind of shrugged.

"Look, Joe," he said. He sounded real tired all of a sudden. "I'm busy. I'm sorry. Go home, will you? I can't take your letter."

"Sure you can," I said. "It's got a stamp on it." What was the matter with him anyway? He was starting to pick up all those boxes again, so I just put it on this table where there were about a million letters and I walked out.

"I'll be back pretty soon," I said. "Tomorrow. I guess there'll be an answer by tomorrow for sure."

I could hardly wait, thinking how surprised my mother was going to be and everything. So the next day, as soon as the school bus let me out at the corner at noon, I ran down to the post office. There were some other people moving boxes around in this big room, so I just kind of walked around the edge until I saw him in another little empty room. He was sitting on a box, eating his lunch.

"Did I get a letter yet?" I said. I was kind of out of breath. He let out a big groan when he saw me standing there, and he kept right on eating this big sandwich. His face was still dirty. He looked madder than ever.

Pretty soon he gave this big sigh, like my father once when I cut up his pajamas for a Halloween costume. "As a matter of fact," he said, "a letter did turn up this morning addressed to somebody named 'Joe.' And nobody . . . nobody . . . could have been more surprised than I was."

"I knew it!" I said. "I told you so!" It was for me, all right. I could see my name "Joe" on the envelope, but there was a lot of writing, like typewriting, on the paper inside, so I gave it back to him. I was in a hurry.

"I can't read writing very well," I said. "You read it. Hurry up! I told you he was coming home."

"Now wait a minute, Joe," he said. "Let's wait and see what the letter says."

I could hardly wait. I kept kind of jumping up and down, I was in such a hurry. "Sit down, will you?" he said.

I sat down on this box beside him. He began to read kind of fast and running the words together:

Dear Joe:

Thank you for your letter. I wish I could make sure that your father would be home for Christmas but I'm afraid I can't, so please don't count on it. However, I hope you have a Merry Christmas.

Very truly yours,

Santa Claus

"Is that all?" I said. "There must be more. Maybe you dropped the other part somewhere. Look around, will you?"

He let out another big groan. "As a matter of fact," he said, "now that you mention it, I guess I did forget one thing. Some marbles turned up here this morning addressed to somebody named 'Joe.' I guess they're for you too."

He reached in his pocket and pulled out this sack of marbles. Boy, they were real good marbles and everything, and I was sure glad to get them. But I was still worried about the letter. "I guess I better hurry up and write another letter," I said. "You can mail it for me like you did before. I guess I didn't say how important it was. Anyway, I want to thank him for the marbles."

"That won't be necessary," he said. "I give you my personal guarantee that there is no point in writing another letter."

"This time you write it," I said. "You can make it sound better. Thank him for the marbles and tell him how important it is that my father comes home, and not to forget the rest of the things I'm supposed to get, like the baseball glove and the football and the electric train. Mail it right away, will you?"

"Joe," he said, "you're a determined man. So am I. Right now I am eating my lunch." He took out this big ham sandwich.

"Is that a ham sandwich?" I said.

"Yes," he said.

"Is it good?" I said.

"Yes," he said. He looked at me kind of mad and he kept on chewing real hard, and then he took another ham sandwich out of the bag. "Could I possibly persuade you to join me?" he said.

"Sure," I said. It was good too. I was hungry.

"What's your name?" I said.

"Al," he said.

Pretty soon we finished the sandwiches. Then he took out this big red apple and started to eat it.

"My father used to cut up apples with his penknife," I said.

"I'll bet he did," Al said. "I'll bet he had to, in self-defense."

I watched Al cut up the apple, and we ate it for awhile.

"How come you don't want to write this letter for me?" I said. "Don't you know how to write a letter?"

All of a sudden Al threw the apple core clear out the door to the alley.

"I know how to write a letter, all right," he said. "I just don't know how to get the right answers." Maybe there was a worm in the apple or something. He sure looked funny.

"How come?" I said. "You mean, you don't think you're going to get what you want for Christmas either?"

"You might put it that way," Al said. "Only in the Army we called it a 'Dear John' letter."

Boy, did he look crabby all of a sudden, like this big lion, the time my father took me to the zoo, that had a toothache and tried to bite everybody.

"What's a 'Dear John' letter?" I said. "Is it good or bad?" I guess it was this letter that made him look so mad all the time, all right. Now he picked up an orange and threw it out the door, without even eating it or anything. What was the matter with him, anyway?

"Let's just skip it, Joe," he said pretty soon. "All it means is that a girl married somebody else."

"Girls are sure dumb," I said. "Playing with dolls and kissing people and everything. I hate girls."

"Hold that thought, Joe," Al said. "It may come in handy later on."

"If you're in the Army, how come you work in the post office?" I said.

"I got rotated home last month," Al said. "I needed a job. The post office needed an extra clerk for the Christmas rush. We were made for each other."

He crumpled up his lunch bag and threw it out the door. Boy, he sure had a good aim. I bet he could of been a big-league pitcher or something if he wanted to. "Look, Joe," he said. "Recess is over. If you have plans for this afternoon, don't let me detain you."

"Well, I guess I better get home, on account of Mrs. Henderson will have a fit," I said. "Don't forget to write the letter right away. Make it a good one. I'll be back tomorrow."

Al kind of groaned again, like my father the time my white rat made a nest in his bedroom slipper.

"Look, Joe," he said, "we've just been through all this. Take my word for it, it's a lost cause. I can't possibly write the letter."

"Sure you can," I said. "I'll pay you back for the stamp and everything out of this money I saved up for Christmas. Send it airmail."

I came right back after school the next day, and Al was eating his lunch again in this kind of empty room. He didn't even look up when I came in. He was eating a fried-egg sandwich.

"Where's the letter?" I said. "Does it say my father is coming for sure?"

Al just kept on eating. He had kind of a fried-egg mustache.

"Didn't it come yet?" I said. "There's only one more day until Christmas."

"Look, Joe," Al said. "Let's not kid ourselves. I told you there wouldn't be any letter."

"Maybe it just didn't get here yet," I said. "Wasn't there even a bag or a box or anything, like last time when he sent the marbles?"

Al let out this big long sigh. "As a matter of fact," he said, "now that you mention it, I do

remember finding this paper bag with your name on it. There seems to be some kind of big glove in it." He gave me this old wrinkled paper bag.

"That's the baseball glove!" I said. "Don't you even know that?" Boy, was he dumb. It was about a million times too big, but it was sure a good glove. "That's one of the things I'm supposed to get for Christmas," I said. "Don't you remember? I already told you. There were the marbles and the baseball glove and a football and an electric train . . ."

"I know," Al said. "Just don't keep reminding me."

"Is that a fried-egg sandwich?" I said.

Al gave it to me and took out another one.

"Joe, I'm eating my lunch," he said. "I mean, we're eating my lunch. Don't you ever get anything to eat at school?"

"You're not supposed to eat anything at school!" I said. He sure didn't know anything. "You're supposed to learn things. Didn't you ever go to school?"

"Off and on," Al said. "What things are you supposed to learn?"

"Drawing and things," I said. "I'm in kindergarten. What were you supposed to learn?"

"Drawing and things," Al said. "I was going to be an architect."

"I bet that would be fun," I said. "What is it?"

"It's somebody who builds things," Al said. "Like houses and so forth." He took out this big banana and peeled it, and I helped him eat it.

"I sure wish we had a house," I said. "Can you build one?"

"First you have to learn how," Al said.

"Then why don't you learn how?" I said.

All of a sudden Al threw the banana peel clear out the door to the alley. He was beginning to look mad again. "Look, Joe," he said. "It's a long grind. That was a long time ago. I had a lot of plans then that never worked out." All of a sudden he took out this big candy bar and ate the whole thing before I could even say anything. "I've got a whole new set of problems now," he said. "Like finding another job after Christmas."

"What kind of job?" I said.

"Any kind of job," Al said. "Who cares? What difference does it make?"

"You're sure you don't want to build a house?" I said. "So you could have a dog in the backyard and everything? I sure like dogs."

All of a sudden Al threw the whole lunch bag out the door, without even eating the rest of it or anything. "Look, Joe," he said. "I don't want to build a house. I don't want to be an architect. I don't want to have a dog in the backyard."

Boy, he sure did look crabby now, like that big lion at the zoo when that man tried to fix his toothache, that kept roaring and jumping up and biting people. "Listen, Joe," he said. "I've got to get back to work. You've got to go home. Let's just skip the whole thing. Go play with your marbles."

So then he went back in this big room with all the boxes, and he went inside one of these cages where people sell stamps and everything. He shut the door, but I could tell which cage it was on account of it said STAMPS on the glass bar. There wasn't hardly anybody in this big room, so I went around the edge until I got to his door and I opened it real quiet. There were about a million people lined up on the other side of the cage, waiting to buy some stamps and everything.

"Hey, Al," I said. "We forgot to look for the letter. I'll come back tomorrow and help you find it."

Al turned around and looked at me. He looked madder than ever. I mean, real mad, like my father the time I dropped his watch in the bathtub. "Let's face it, Joe," he said. "There isn't going to be any letter. I'm sorry, but sometimes you just don't get what you want for Christmas."

"You do if you want it hard enough," I said. "My father said so. He said we would have a real big Christmas tree this year, and underneath there would be the marbles and the baseball glove and the football and the . . ."

"Listen, Joe," Al said. "I've done all I can. I'm sorry, believe me. Run along now, will you? Get lost. I just haven't got any more time to play games."

Who asked him to play games, anyway? All of a sudden the door to the cage shut with a bang right in front of me. I guess it blew shut or something. So I went home.

The next day it was Christmas Eve, only not until that night, you know what I mean. I didn't get to go to the post office after school, on account of Mrs. Henderson picked me up, but pretty soon I sneaked out while she was baking some cookies and she thought I was taking a nap.

I guess it was pretty late, all right; it was almost dark by the time I got there. It was sure cold. The back door to the post office was locked. I couldn't even open it. So I came around the side and there was somebody sitting on the steps. It was Al. He still looked mad, like my father the time I got lost at the circus. He was sort of shivering and his face looked kind of blue. "What are you doing here?" he said. "You're late."

"I was looking for you," I said. "My mother said last night that my father really isn't going to come home for Christmas, no matter what. She said I shouldn't of bothered you. I'm sorry I bothered you."

"Think nothing of it," Al said. "Everything bothers me." He gave me this kind of lumpy-looking big bag. "I just thought I'd better make sure you got this package that came for you today. It looks like it's got some kind of a ball in it."

"That's a football!" I said. Boy, it was a real football, like they use in a football game and everything. "Thanks for waiting," I said. I sat down beside him on the steps. It was pretty cold, all right.

"Joe," Al said, "why don't you go home?" He looked like my father the time I put this real swell lizard I found once on his plate at dinner. "Doesn't anybody pay any attention to where you are?"

"Sure they pay attention," I said. "They think I'm asleep. My mother has to work late tonight, until nine o'clock in the store, and she said afterward she's going to go out again and get the Christmas tree. Only the thing is, I'm going to surprise her. I'm going to get this big tree and put it up like my father always does, so we can put the electric train under it."

"*What* electric train?" Al said.

"The one I wrote about in the letter. Only it hasn't got here yet."

"I wouldn't count on it," Al said. "You can't be too sure about getting things. For example, you need an electric train, but I need a new suit. One of us is apt to be disappointed."

"It'll come, all right," I said. "Everything else did. It'll probably be there when I get back home. Do you like to pick out Christmas trees and put the ornaments on and everything?"

"No," Al said.

"I never bought a Christmas tree before," I said. "I went with my father. But I guess it's easy, all right."

"Have you got any money?"

"Sure I've got money," I said. I guess he thought I was dumb or something. "I had almost a dollar saved up, and I spent fifty cents for a present for mother, so I've got thirty-five cents left."

All of a sudden Al looked like he was getting mad again, or tired or something. "Look, Joe, just go home, will you?" he said. "Forget about the Christmas tree and the electric train. Get a good night's sleep."

"I will," I said. "First I want to get the tree, so I can put the electric train under it."

I started down this street where I saw this big place where they sell Christmas trees, but I couldn't hardly even see the post office, it was too dark. So I kept on going.

Pretty soon I heard somebody in back of me. It was Al. "Hey, Joe!" he said. He had this kind of funny look on his face, like my father the time I made this big Father's Day card for him at school and brought it home. "I just happened to think of a fellow I know who sells Christmas trees," Al said. "I saw some big ones there for about thirty-five cents."

"Well, it was down this way," Al said. "But if you don't mind waiting, I've got an errand to do first in the hardware store."

Al told me to wait outside the hardware store, and he was in there for a pretty long time, but I didn't mind waiting on account of there was this electric train set up in the window with tracks and bridges and tunnels and everything. It sure was a swell train.

It was a good thing Al came along when I bought this Christmas tree at this place he knew for thirty-five cents, on account of I couldn't even carry the tree, it was so big. Al had to carry it. I helped him some. It sure smelled good.

It was a pretty long walk home. By the time we got there this truck was stopped out in front and a man was just putting a big box in front of our door in the hall.

"That's my electric train," I said. "I told you it would get here."

"That's right," Al said. "Now that I think of it, you did tell me."

Mrs. Henderson was sure mad when she saw I had sneaked out and everything, but Al said he would get me some supper, so after awhile she unlocked the door to our apartment and we went inside. Boy, the tree I bought was too big, even, but it fitted fine after Al cut off the top of the tree like my father used to do.

It turned out this electric train was so big it ran all around the living room. First we put down the tracks and the bridges and the tunnels and the trestle and the freight cars and the engine and the passenger train and the caboose. Then Al put all these ornaments we had on the tree while I put the marbles and the baseball glove and the football underneath, like they were supposed to be.

He had just put this big star on the top of the tree when my mother came in. Boy, was she surprised. She looked kind of tired and messed up and she was carrying all these packages.

"This is Al," I said.

My mother looked at Al and he looked at her, and all of a sudden they kind of smiled. Her face got all red and she sort of just stood there.

"Well, this certainly is kind of you," my mother said. Her voice sure sounded funny. "Joe has told me so much about you. I don't know how to thank you."

Al started to climb down off the kitchen stool and he sort of fell down the last step. "It was a real pleasure," he said, real polite and everything. He sounded kind of funny too. "I really enjoy trimming a Christmas tree."

What was the matter with him, anyway? He didn't like to trim Christmas trees. "Well, I'll be on my way now," he said. "I'm very glad to have met you."

"Oh, do you have to hurry off?" my mother said. "I'm sure Joe would like you to stay." Boy, her face was sure pink. All of a sudden, she didn't look so tired. "I've brought home some fruitcake and I'll just put on some coffee. It won't take a minute. Won't you sit down?"

My mother sat down in a chair. Al sat down in another chair.

"I understand you work in the post office," my mother said. "That must be interesting work."

"Well, it's only temporary, of course," Al said. "I'm thinking of going back to study architecture. That's the career I'm really interested in, building and all."

What did he say that for? He didn't like building at all. "Hey, Al," I said. "How come . . ."

My mother got up and went into the kitchen and started to make some coffee. Pretty soon you could smell the coffee and the Christmas tree all together. It sure smelled good. Al turned on the Christmas tree lights and then he built a fire in the fireplace and then he made the train go. It ran all over the room, under the bridges and over the mountains and through the tunnels. I never saw such a good train.

Pretty soon my mother started to bring in a lot of things to eat, like when we had a party with my father, in front of the fire. Her face was all pink, and she kept on smiling and everything. She sure looked nice.

"Do you live around here?" she asked Al.

"Yes, I have a room a few blocks away," Al said. "But before too long I want to build a house with a big yard and plenty of room for a dog and all that."

What did he go and say that for? Boy, he sure must have changed his mind or something.

"Hey, Al," I said. "How come . . ."

"Joe," Al said, "there is something I've been meaning to tell you for quite some time."

"What?" I said.

"Merry Christmas," he said.

And that was the night my father came home. ✦

Christmas Memories

Christmas Surprises

Christmas Travels

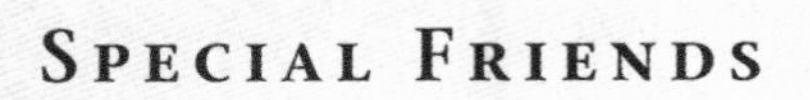

Special Friends

Kitten of Bethlehem

RUTH C. IKERMAN

Kitten was lonely. Have you ever been lonely?
Kitten was afraid. Have you ever been afraid?
Then Kitten heard something!

ALTHOUGH WE SELDOM THINK OF ANIMALS, EXCEPT DONKEYS, LIVING DURING THE TIME OF THE BIRTH OF JESUS, SURELY THEY WERE THERE. RUTH IKERMAN, THE AUTHOR OF THIS STORY, MUST HAVE A DEEP LOVE FOR CATS TO BE ABLE TO WRITE SUCH A SPECIAL STORY WITH A KITTEN AS THE MAIN CHARACTER. ALL ANIMALS ARE ABLE TO SEE THE WORLD FROM A DIFFERENT VIEW THAN WE AS HUMANS SEE IT. THIS KITTEN MUST HAVE SEEN THINGS THAT EVEN JOSEPH AND MARY DIDN'T SEE. WHAT AN EXCITING LIFE FOR A KITTEN!

hen the innkeeper picked up a stone and tossed it at the furry tail, the kitten ran as fast as he could. He didn't stop until he reached the stable behind the inn.

Cautiously he poked his head around the corner to see if there was anyone inside who would make him move on. He was very tired and hungry. The only food he had found all day was a little milk in an indentation of a big rock where the goats had been milked. These belonged to a crowd of people who had just arrived.

There seemed to be lots of people coming into the town just now, with official-looking men bustling about to count them and their possessions. Kitten had played around the courtyard of the busy inn, hoping some of the strangers would stop to feed him, or at least notice him.

Now the innkeeper himself had shouted at him to get out of the way, and Kitten had barely managed to reach the stable. With his bright eyes, which could see well in the dark, he looked around

to find out who was there ahead of him. Good! Here was a cow, and sometimes a little cat could make friends with a cow. If he stayed close when the good, rich milk was being taken, there might be some for him too.

Over in the stable corner was the sturdy ox with his mate. A mother hen had gathered her chicks under her wings, and they were resting in the straw.

Silently surveying the leap it would be from the dusty ground to the warm manger straw, Kitten paused for strength, for he was weak from hunger. He took a big breath—then with a quick twist of his back feet he took off in a broad jump, and landed nimbly in the sweet-smelling hay. He treaded his bed with his front paws, then dropped his furry face in a moment of surrender and rest.

But soon he heard someone entering the stable. Could the innkeeper be hunting him? He jumped up and arched his back, making his tail twice its usual size. At least he would put up a good fight if the big dogs were turned loose on him.

Instead, Kitten saw a tired little donkey entering the stable—the same kind of patient animal that had been bringing people into the inn courtyard. Kitten let his tail return to normal size before he scampered forward to welcome the newcomer. He knew what it was to be lonely and afraid, and he wanted to offer his friendship.

The donkey looked at him out of one big eye beneath a big ear, and the kitten looked back out of his eyes which could see in the dark. He said, "Welcome," in the sweetest tone of meow he could manage in his hunger.

The donkey halted as the man walking beside him said, "It's all right. Here we are now, with a roof over our heads, and shelter for the night."

The man was speaking to a woman seated on the donkey. Tenderly he lifted her down to the manger, and she gave a soft sigh of relief on reaching the straw. She closed her eyes and put her head back on the pillow of hay.

Kitten had never seen such a sweet, kind face. He crept closer. His paws moved a stray piece of straw that tickled the lady's arm. She opened her eyes and saw the kitten beside her. Gently the soft hands touched his head, and he felt the fear going out of him at the touch.

Holding fast to the kitten, she reached out to the man beside the donkey and said, "Oh, see what we have found! A beautiful kitten waiting with us for our baby."

Suddenly the lonely kitten felt he was within the circle of a family. His heart pounded with the sheer joy of knowing that now he belonged to someone.

The man reached into the bag that hung from the side of the donkey and took out a little brown earthen bowl. Into it, he poured milk from a skin container. He crumbled a piece of brown bread into the liquid. Then he placed it on the ground and beckoned to the kitten.

How good the bread and milk tasted! Kitten tried not to take it all in greedy gulps. Methodically he cleaned the bowl, then withdrew on soft feet to the corner of the stable, and soon was asleep.

When Kitten opened his eyes, he thought it must be morning, but the light which streamed into the open manger was not like any sunlight he had ever seen. Yet it was not like the night either, although there were stars overhead—the same stars under which he had traveled, weary and alone, hunting a home.

An unusual radiance streamed from the largest star of all, directly over the manger. And there lay a baby cradled beside the lady with the understanding eyes. Nearby stood the man, the weariness erased from his face in a moment of happy triumph over discouragement.

The cow chewed her cud rhythmically, and the breath of the oxen came in deep measures of satisfaction. A white chicken clucked and the others answered drowsily. Soon all were wide awake, for glorious music filled the stable.

It seemed to Kitten that the light was singing. Such heavenly sounds he had never heard before. He felt he would burst if he couldn't join the hallelujahs of joy.

Kitten had never learned to sing, but he wanted to be part of this chorus. He took a deep breath and let the good air come into his tiny lungs. He began to purr in time with the song he heard. Louder swelled the chorus from on high. It was echoed in Kitten's sweet, harmonious purring.

The mother turned from looking at her child and saw again the kitten, his little ribs pressing out as he purred his lullaby for the new baby. She smiled at Kitten, and over him passed such a peace as he had never expected to find on this earth.

Thinking of the gifts he would find for the new baby, he looked up to see a white lamb approaching ahead of a shepherd with a crook. Kitten had seen such men in the hills, and sometimes one would share his food with a wandering kitten. Now a band of shepherds approached the manger as though guided by the star. They knelt and offered the beautiful lamb as a love gift.

Watching the shepherds presenting their gift to the baby, Kitten turned away in discouragement. What gift could he bring to the baby? He remembered the gentle touch of the beautiful lady, and the kindness of the man in sharing their food. There must be something he could give in return.

Deep in his heart he said, I do not have anything to give except myself. I will give that gladly. He moved to the foot of the manger and climbed the rough wood to the straw. He stretched out the full length of his furry coat to let its warmth comfort the tired feet of the lady, resting with the child in her arms. She put her head back and smiled. Kitten felt his heart warmed within him. His gift had been accepted in love, even as it had been offered.

He began to purr again in gratitude. He had found the rich satisfaction and peace that come from giving of oneself. Happily he closed his eyes to sleep, and to gather strength for the living of his new life, which would be forever marked by the echo of the wonderful song. ✦

Traditions to Help Others

Pets at Christmas

Trouble at the Inn

DINA DONOHUE

Wally the innkeeper was stern. Let them in?
No way—not in a thousand years!
He started to close the door . . .

WALLY WAS OLDER THAN HIS CLASSMATES, AND TALLER TOO. THAT'S WHY HE WAS A SHOO-IN FOR THE ROLE OF HARD-HEARTED INNKEEPER IN THE SCHOOL NATIVITY PLAY. AND HE FOLLOWED THE SCRIPT IN ALL THEIR PRACTICES, BUT SOMETHING HAPPENED BETWEEN THE PRACTICE AND THE PERFORMANCE. SO, AFTER YOU HEAR THE STORY READ, ASK YOURSELF WHY THIS SIMPLE LITTLE STORY OF BOYS AND GIRLS IN BATHROBES AND SHEETS HAS BECOME SO GREATLY LOVED. WHAT REASONS CAN YOU THINK OF?

or years now whenever Christmas pageants are talked about in a certain little town in the Midwest, someone is sure to mention the name of Wallace Purling. Wally's performance in one annual production of the Nativity play has slipped into the realm of legend. But the old-timers who were in the audience that night never tire of recalling exactly what happened.

Wally was nine that year and in the second grade, though he should have been in the fourth. Most people in town knew that he had difficulty in keeping up. He was big and clumsy, slow in movement and mind. Still, Wally was well liked by the other children in his class, all of whom were smaller than he, though the boys had trouble hiding their irritation when the uncoordinated Wally would ask to play ball with them.

Most often they'd find a way to keep him off the field, but Wally would hang around anyway—not sulking, just hoping. He was

always a helpful boy, a willing and smiling one, and the natural protector, paradoxically, of the underdog. Sometimes if the older boys chased the younger ones away, it would always be Wally who'd say, "Can't they stay? They're no bother."

Wally fancied the idea of being a shepherd with a flute in the Christmas pageant that year, but the play's director, Miss Lumbard, assigned him to a more important role. After all, she reasoned, the Innkeeper did not have too many lines, and Wally's size would make his refusal of lodging to Joseph more forceful.

And so it happened that the usual large, partisan audience gathered for the town's Yuletide extravaganza of the crooks and creches, of beards, crowns, halos and a whole stageful of squeaky voices. No one on stage or off was more caught up in the magic of the night than Wallace Purling. They said later that he stood in the wings and watched the performance with such fascination that from time to time Miss Lumbard had to make sure he didn't wander onstage before his cue.

Then the time came when Joseph appeared, slowly, tenderly guiding Mary to the door of the inn. Joseph knocked hard on the wooden door set into the painted backdrop. Wally the Innkeeper was there, waiting.

"What do you want?" Wally said, swinging the door open with a brusque gesture.

"We seek lodging."

"Seek it elsewhere." Wally looked straight ahead but spoke vigorously. "The inn is filled."

"Sir, we have asked everywhere in vain. We have traveled far and are very weary."

"There is no room in this inn for you." Wally looked properly stern.

"Please, good Innkeeper, this is my wife, Mary. She is heavy with child and needs a place to rest. Surely you must have some small corner for her. She is so tired."

Now for the first time, the Innkeeper relaxed his stiff stance and looked down at Mary. With that, there was a long pause, long enough to make the audience a bit tense with embarrassment.

"No! Begone!" the prompter whispered from the wings.

"No!" Wally repeated automatically. "Begone!"

Joseph sadly placed his arm around Mary and Mary laid her head upon her husband's shoulder and the two of them started to move away. The Innkeeper did not return inside his inn, however. Wally stood there in the doorway, watching the forlorn couple. His mouth was open, his brow creased with concern, his eyes filling unmistakably with tears.

And suddenly this Christmas pageant became different from all others.

"Don't go, Joseph," Wally called out. "Bring Mary back." And Wallace Purling's face grew into a bright smile. "You can have my room."

Some people in town thought that the pageant had been ruined. Yet there were others—many, many others—who considered it the most Christmas of all Christmas pageants they had ever seen. ✦

Christmas Memories

FAMILY PHOTOS

Favorite Family Activities

A Certain Small Shepherd

REBECCA CAUDILL

Everything other little children could do, Jamie could do—except for one thing. He could not talk. Then came the terrible storm!

REBECCA CAUDILL REALLY KNEW THE PEOPLE WHO LIVED IN THE MOUNTAINS OF APPALACHIA. HAVE YOU EVER WONDERED WHAT IT WOULD BE LIKE IF SOMEONE ASKED YOU A QUESTION, AND YOU COULDN'T TALK? WELL, LISTEN CAREFULLY AND YOU'LL FIND OUT WHAT IT WOULD BE LIKE. WHAT'S EXTRA SPECIAL ABOUT THIS STORY IS THAT, EVEN THOUGH JAIME CAN'T TALK, THE THOUGHTS SOUND LIKE WHAT HE WOULD HAVE SAID IF HE COULD TALK. OVER THE YEARS, THIS STORY HAS GRADUALLY BECOME A CHRISTMAS CLASSIC. THE AUTHOR, REBECCA CAUDILL, WAS BORN IN 1899 IN POOR FORK, KENTUCKY. IN THIS, AND OTHER STORIES SHE WROTE, HER BELOVED KENTUCKY HILLS LIVE AGAIN.

This is a story of a strange and marvelous thing. It happened on a Christmas morning, at Hurricane Gap, and not so long ago at that.

But before you hear about Christmas morning, you must hear about Christmas Eve, for that is part of the story.

And before you hear about Christmas Eve, you must hear about Jamie, for without Jamie there would be no story.

Jamie was born on a freakish night in November. The cold that night moved down from the North and rested its heavy hand suddenly on Hurricane Gap. Within an hour's time the naked earth turned brittle.

Line Fork Creek froze solid in its winding bed and lay motionless, like a string dropped at the foot of Pine Mountain.

Nothing but the dark wind was abroad in the hollow. Wild creatures huddled in their dens. Cows stood hunched in their stalls. Housewives stuffed the cracks underneath their doors against the needling cold, and men heaped oak and apple wood on their fires.

At the foot of the Gap where Jamie's house stood, the wind doubled its fury. It battered the doors of the house. It rattled the windows. It wailed like a banshee in the chimney. "For sure it's bad luck trying to break in," moaned Jamie's mother, and turned her face to her pillow.

"Bad luck has no business here," Jamie's father said bravely. He laid more logs on the fire. Flames licked at them and roared up the chimney. But through the roaring the wind wailed on thin and high.

Father took the newborn baby from the bed beside its mother and sat holding it on his knee. "Saro," he called, "you and Honey come and see Jamie!"

Two girls came from the shadows of the room. In the firelight they stood looking at the tiny, wrinkled, red face inside the blanket.

"He's such a little brother!" said Saro.

"Give him time, he'll grow," said Father proudly. "When he's three, he'll be as big as Honey. When he's six, he'll be as big as you. You want to hold him?"

Saro sat down on the stool and Father laid the bundle in her arms.

Honey stood beside Saro. She pulled back the corner of the blanket. She opened one of the tiny hands and laid one of her fingers in it. She smiled at the face in the blanket. She looked upward, smiling at Father.

But Father did not see her. He was standing beside Mother, trying to comfort her.

That night Jamie's mother died.

Jamie ate and slept and grew.

Like other babies, he cut teeth. He learned to sit alone, and to crawl. When he was a year old, he toddled about like other one-year-olds. At two, he carried around sticks and stones like other two-year-olds. He threw balls, and built towers of blocks and knocked them down.

Everything that other two-year-olds could do Jamie could do, except one thing. He could not talk.

The women of Hurricane Gap sat in their chimney corners and shook their heads.

"His mother, poor soul, should have rubbed him with lard," said one.

"She ought to have brushed him with a rabbit's foot," said another.

"Wasn't the boy born on a Wednesday?" asked another. "Wednesday's child is full of woe," she quoted from an old saying.

"Jamie gets everything he wants by pointing," explained Father. "Give him time. He'll learn to talk."

At three, Jamie could zip his pants and tie his shoes.

At four, he followed Father to the stable and milked the kittens' pan full of milk. But even at four, Jamie could not talk like other children. He could only make strange grunting noises.

One day Jamie found a litter of new kittens in a box under the stairs. He ran to the cornfield to tell Father. He wanted to say he had been feeling around in the box for a ball he'd lost, and suddenly his fingers felt something warm and squirmy, and there were all those kittens. But how could you tell somebody something if when you opened your mouth you could only grunt?

Jamie started running. He ran till he reached the orchard. There he threw himself facedown in the tall grass and kicked his feet against the ground.

One day Honey's friend came to play hide-and-seek. Jamie played with them. Because Clive was the oldest, he shut his eyes first and counted to fifty while the other children scattered and hid behind trees in the yard and corners of the house. After he had counted to fifty, the hollow rang with cries.

"One, two, three for Millie!"

"One, two, three for Jamie!"

"One, two, three for Honey!"

"One, two, three—I'm home free."

It came Jamie's turn to shut his eyes. He sat on the doorstep, covered his eyes with his hands and began to count.

"Listen to Jamie!" Clive called to the other children. The others listened. They all began to laugh.

Jamie got up from the doorstep. He ran after the children. He fought them with both fists and both feet. Honey helped him.

Then Jamie ran away to the orchard and threw himself down on his face in the tall grass and kicked the ground.

Later, when Father was walking through the orchard, he came across Jamie lying in the grass.

"Jamie," said Father, "there's a new calf in the pasture. I need you to help me bring it to the stable."

Jamie got up from the grass. He wiped his eyes. Out of the orchard and across the pasture he trudged at Father's heels. In a far corner of the pasture, they found the cow. Beside her, on wobbly legs, stood the new calf.

Together Father and Jamie drove the cow and the calf to the stable, into an empty stall. Together they brought nubbins from the corncrib to feed the cow. Together they made a bed of clean hay for the calf.

"Jamie," said Father the next morning, "I need you to help plow the corn." Father harnessed the horse and lifted Jamie to the horse's back. Away to the cornfield they went, Father walking in front of the horse; Jamie riding, holding tight to the mane.

While Father plowed, Jamie walked in the furrow behind him. When Father lay on his back in the shade of the persimmon tree to rest, Jamie lay beside him. Father told Jamie the names of the birds flying overhead: the turkey vulture lifting and tilting its uplifted wings against the white clouds, the carrion crow flapping lazily and sailing, and the sharp-shinned hawk gliding to rest in the woodland.

The next day, Jamie helped Father set out sweet potatoes. Other days he helped Father trim fence rows and mend fences. Whatever Father did, Jamie helped him.

One day Father drove the car out of the shed and stopped in front of the house.

"Jamie!" he called. "Jump in. We're going across Pine Mountain."

"Can I go too?" asked Honey.

"Not today," said Father. "I'm taking Jamie to see a doctor."

The doctor looked at Jamie's throat. He listened to Jamie grunt. He shook his head.

"You might see Dr. Jones," he said.

Father and Jamie got into the car and drove across Big Black Mountain to see Dr. Jones.

"Maybe Jamie could learn to talk," said Dr. Jones. "But he would have to be sent away to a special school. He would have to stay there several months. He might even have to stay two or three years. Or four."

"It is a long time," said Dr. Jones.

"And the pocket is empty," said Father.

So Father and Jamie got into the car and started home. Usually Father talked to Jamie as they drove along. Now they drove all the way, across Big Black and across Pine, without a word.

In August, every year, school opened at Hurricane Gap. On the first morning of school, the year that Jamie was six, Father handed him a book, a tablet, a pencil and a box of crayons, all shiny and new.

"You're going to school, Jamie," he said. "I'll go with you this morning."

The neighbors watched them walking down the road together, toward the little one-room schoolhouse.

"Poor, foolish Father!" they said, and shook their heads. "Trying to make somebody out of that no-account boy!"

Miss Creech, the teacher, shook her head too. With so many children, so many classes, so many grades, she hadn't time for a boy that couldn't talk, she told Father.

"What will Jamie do all day long?" she asked.

"He will listen," said Father.

So Jamie took his tablet, his pencil and his book of crayons, and sat down in an empty seat in the front row.

Every day Jamie listened. He learned the words in the pages of his book. He learned how to count. He liked the reading and counting. But the part of school Jamie liked best was the big piece of paper Miss Creech gave him every day. On it he printed words in squares, like the other children. He wrote numbers. He drew pictures and colored them with his crayons. He could say things on paper.

One day Miss Creech said Jamie had the best paper in the first grade. She held it up for all the children to see.

On sunny days on the playground the children played ball games and three deep and duck-on-a-rock: games a boy can play without talking. On rainy days they played indoors.

One rainy day the children played a guessing game. Jamie knew the answer that no other child could guess. But he couldn't say the answer. He didn't know how to spell the answer. He could only point to show that he knew the answer.

That evening at home he threw his book into the corner. He slammed the door. He pulled Honey's hair. He twisted the cat's tail. The cat yowled and leaped under the bed.

"Jamie," said Father, "cats have feelings, just like boys."

Every year the people of Hurricane Gap celebrated Christmas in the white-steepled church that stood across the road from Jamie's house. On Christmas Eve the boys and girls gave a Christmas play. People came miles to see it, from the other side of Pine Mountain and from the head of every creek and hollow. Miss Creech directed the play.

Through the late fall, as the leaves fell from the trees and the days grew shorter and the air snapped with cold, Jamie wondered when Miss Creech would talk about the play. Finally, one

afternoon in November, Miss Creech announced it was time to begin play practice.

Jamie laid his book inside the desk and listened carefully as Miss Creech assigned the parts of the play.

Miss Creech gave the part of Mary to Joan who lived up in Pine Mountain beyond the rock quarry. She asked Honey to bring her big doll to be the baby. She gave the part of Joseph to Henry who lived at the head of Little Laurelpatch. She asked Saro to be an angel, Clive the innkeeper. She chose three big boys to be people living in Bethlehem. The rest of the boys and girls would sing carols, she said.

Jamie for a moment listened to the sound of the words he had heard. Yes, Miss Creech expected him to sing carols.

Every day after school the boys and girls went with Miss Creech up the road to the church and practiced the Christmas play.

Every day Jamie stood in the front row of the carolers. The first day he stood quietly. The second day he shoved Milly who was standing next to him. The third day he pulled Honey's hair. The fourth day, when the carolers began singing, Jamie ran to the window, grabbed a ball from the sill and bounced it across the floor.

"Wait a minute, children," Miss Creech said to the children. She turned to Jamie.

"Jamie," she asked, "how would you like to be a shepherd?"

"He's too little," said one of the big shepherds.

"No, he isn't," said Saro. "If my father was a shepherd, Jamie would help him."

That afternoon Jamie became a small shepherd. He ran home after practice to tell father. Father couldn't understand what Jamie was telling him, but he knew that Jamie had been changed into somebody important.

One afternoon, at play practice, Miss Creech said to the boys and girls, "Forget you are Joan and Henry and Saro and Clive and Jamie. Remember that you are Mary and Joseph, an angel, an innkeeper, and a shepherd, and that strange things are happening in the hollow where you live."

That night at bedtime, Father took the big Bible off the table. Saro and Honey and Jamie gathered around the fire. Over the room a hush fell as Father read: "And there were in the same country shepherds abiding in the fields, keeping watch over their flocks by night. And lo, the angel of the Lord came upon them, and the glory of the Lord shone around about them: and they were sore afraid. And the angel said unto them, Fear not: for, behold, I bring you good tidings of great joy which shall be to all people . . . And it came to pass, as the angels were gone away from them into heaven, the shepherds said to one another, Let us now go even until Bethlehem, and see this thing which is come to pass, which the Lord hath made known unto us. And they came with haste, and found Mary and Joseph, and the babe lying in a manger."

Christmas drew near. At home in the evenings, when they had finished studying their lessons, the boys and girls of Hurricane Gap made decorations for the Christmas tree that would stand in the church. They glued together strips of bright-colored paper in long chains. They whittled stars and baby lambs and camels out of wild cherry wood. They strung long strings of popcorn.

Jamie strung a string of popcorn. Every night as Father read from the Bible, Jamie added more kernels to his string.

"Jamie, are you trying to make a string long enough to reach to the top of Pine Mountain?" asked Honey one night.

Jamie did not hear her. He was far away on a hillside, tending sheep. And even though he was a small shepherd and could only grunt when he tried to talk, an angel wrapped around with dazzling light was singling him out to tell him a wonderful thing had happened down in the hollow in a cow stall. He fell asleep, stringing his popcorn and listening.

In a corner of the room where the fire burned, Father pulled from under his bed the trundle bed in which Jamie slept. He turned back the covers, picked Jamie up from the floor and laid him gently in the bed.

The next day Father went across Pine Mountain to the store. When he came home, he handed Saro a package. In it was cloth of four colors: green, gold, white and red.

"Make Jamie a shepherd's coat, like the picture in the Bible," Father said to Saro.

Father went into the woods and found a crooked limb of a tree. He made it into a shepherd's crook for Jamie.

Jamie went to school the next morning carrying his shepherd's crook and his shepherd's coat on his arm. He would wear his coat and carry his crook when the boys and girls practiced the play.

All day Jamie waited patiently to practice the play. All day he sat listening. But who could tell whose voice he heard? It might have been Miss Creech's. It might have been an angel's.

Two days before Christmas, Jamie's father and Clive's father drove in a pickup truck along the Trace Branch Road, looking for a Christmas tree. On the mountainside they spotted a Juniper growing broad and tall and free. With axes they cut it down. They snaked it down the mountainside and loaded it into the truck.

Father had opened the doors of the church wide to get the tree inside. It reached to the ceiling.

Frost-blue berries shone on its feathery green branches. The air around it smelled of spice.

That afternoon the mothers of Hurricane Gap, and Miss Creech, and all the boys and girls gathered at the church to decorate the tree.

In the tiptop of the tree they fastened the biggest star. Among the branches they hung other stars, and baby lambs and the camels whittled out of wild cherry wood. They hung chains from branch to branch. Last of all, they festooned the tree with strings of snowy popcorn.

"Ah!" they said, as they stood back and looked at the tree. "Ah!"

Beside the tree the boys and girls practiced the Christmas play for the last time. When they had finished, they started home. Midway down the aisle they turned and looked again at the tree.

Saro opened the door. "Look!" she called. "Look, everybody! It's snowing!"

Jamie, the next morning, looked out on a world such as he had never seen. Hidden were the roads and the fences, the woodpile and the swing under the oak tree, all buried deep under a lumpy quilt of snow. And before a stinging wind, snowflakes still madly whirled and danced.

Saro and Honey joined Jamie at the window.

"You can't see across Line Fork Creek in this storm," said Saro. "And where is Pine Mountain?"

"Where is the church?" asked Honey. "That's what I'd like to know."

Jamie turned to them with questions in his eyes.

"If it had been snowing hard that night in Bethlehem, Jamie," Honey told him, "the shepherds wouldn't have had their sheep out in the pasture. They would have had them in the stable, keeping them warm, wouldn't they, Father? They wouldn't have heard what the angel said, all shut indoors like that."

"When angels have something to tell a shepherd," said Father, "they can find him in any place, in any sort of weather. If the shepherd is listening, he will hear."

At eleven o'clock the telephone rang.

"Hello!" said Father.

Saro and Honey and Jamie heard Miss Creech's voice. "I've just got the latest weather

report. This storm is going on all day, and into the night. Do you think . . ."

The telephone started ringing, and once it started to ring it wouldn't stop. Everyone in Hurricane Gap listened. The news they heard was always bad. Drifts ten feet high were piled up along Trace Branch Road. The boys and girls in Little Laurelpatch couldn't get out. Joseph lived in Little Laurelpatch. The road up to the rock quarry. . . Mary couldn't get down the mountain. And then the telephone went silent, dead in the storm.

Meanwhile, the snow kept up its crazy dance before the wind. It drifted in great white mounds across the roads and in the fence rows.

"Nobody but a foolish man would take to the road on a day like this," said Father.

At dinner Jamie sat at the table staring at his plate.

"Shepherds must eat, Jamie," said Father.

"Honey and I don't feel like eating either, Jamie," said Saro. "But see how Honey is eating!"

Still Jamie stared at his plate.

"Know what?" asked Saro. "Because we're all disappointed, we won't save the Christmas stack cake for tomorrow. We'll have a slice today. As soon as you eat your dinner, Jamie."

Still Jamie stared at his plate. He did not touch his food.

"You think that play was real, don't you, Jamie?" said Honey. "It wasn't real. It was just a play we were giving, like some story we'd made up."

Jamie could hold his sobs no longer. His body heaved as he ran to Father. Father laid an arm about Jamie's shoulders.

"Sometimes, Jamie," he said, "angels say to shepherds, 'Be of good courage.'"

On through the short afternoon the storm raged. Father heaped more wood on the fire. Saro sat in front of the fire reading a book. Honey cracked hickory nuts on the stone hearth. Jamie sat.

"Bring the popper, Jamie, and I'll pop some corn for you," said Father.

Jamie shook his head.

"Want me to read to you?" asked Saro.

Jamie shook his head.

"Why don't you help Honey crack hickory nuts? asked Father.

Jamie shook his head.

"Jamie still thinks he's a shepherd," said Honey.

After a while Jamie left the fire and stood at the window, watching the wild storm. He squinted his eyes and stared—he motioned to his father to come and look. Saro and Honey, too, hurried to the window and peered out.

Through the snowdrifts trudged a man, followed by a woman. They were bundled and

buttoned from head to foot, and their faces were lowered against the wind and the flying snowflakes.

"Lord have mercy!" said Father as he watched them turn up the gate.

Around the house the man and the woman made their way to the back door. As Father opened the door to them, a gust of snowladen wind whisked into the kitchen.

"Come in out of the cold," said Father.

The man and the woman stepped inside. They stamped their feet on the kitchen floor and brushed the snow from their clothes. They followed Father into the front room and sat down before the fire in the chairs Father told Saro to bring. Father, too, sat down.

Jamie stood beside Father. Saro and Honey stood behind his chair. The three of them stared at the man and the woman silently.

"Where did you come from?" asked Father.

"The other side of Pine Mountain," said the man.

"Why didn't you stop sooner?" said Father.

"We did stop," the man said. "At three houses. Nobody had room," he said.

Father was silent for a minute. He looked at his own bed and at Jamie's trundle bed underneath it. The man and the woman looked numbly into the fire.

"How far were you going?" asked Father.

"Down Straight Creek," said the man. He jerked his head toward the woman. "To her sister's."

"You'll never get there tonight," Father said.

"Maybe—" said the man. "Maybe there'd be a place in your stable."

"We could lay pallets on the kitchen floor," said Father.

The woman looked at the children. She shook her head. "The stable is better," she said.

"The stable is cold," said Father.

"It will do," said the woman.

When the man and the woman had dried their clothes and warmed themselves, Father led the way to the stable. He carried an armload of quilts and on top of them an old buffalo skin. From his right arm swung a lantern and a milk bucket. "I'll milk while I'm there," he said to Saro. "Get supper ready."

Jamie and Saro and Honey watched from the kitchen window as the three trudged through the snowdrifts to the stable.

It was dark when Father came back to the house.

"How long are the man and the woman going to stay?" asked Honey.

Father hung a teakettle of water on the crane over the fire and went upstairs to find another lantern.

"All night tonight," he said as he came down the stairs. "Maybe longer."

Father hurriedly ate the supper Saro put on the table . . . Then he took in one hand the lighted lantern and a tin bucket filled with supper for the man and the woman.

"I put some Christmas stack cake in the bucket," said Saro.

In his other hand, Father took the teakettle.

"It's cold in that stable," he said as he started out the kitchen door. "Bitter cold."

On the doorstep he turned. "Don't wait up for me," he called back. "I may be gone a good while."

Over the earth darkness thickened. Still the wind blew and the snow whirled. The clock on the mantel struck eight. It ticked solemnly in the quiet house where Saro and Honey and Jamie waited.

"Why doesn't Father come?" complained Honey.

"Why don't you hang up your stocking and go to bed?" asked Saro. "Jamie, it's time to hang up your stocking, too, and go to bed."

Jamie did not answer. He sat staring into the fire.

"That Jamie! He still thinks he's a shepherd," said Honey as she hung her stocking under the mantel.

"Jamie," said Saro, "aren't you going to hang up your stocking and go to bed?" She pulled the trundle bed from beneath Father's bed and turned back the covers. She turned back the covers on Father's bed. She hung up her stocking and followed Honey upstairs.

"Jamie!" she called out.

Still Jamie stared into the fire. A strange feeling was growing inside him. This night was not like other nights, he knew. Something mysterious was going on. He felt afraid.

What was that he heard? The wind? Only the wind?

He lay down on the bed with his clothes on. He dropped off to sleep. A rattling at the door waked him.

He sat upright quickly. He looked around. His heart beat fast. But nothing in the room had changed. Everything was as it had been when he lay down. The fire was burning; two stockings, Saro's and Honey's, hung under the mantel; the clock was ticking solemnly.

He looked at Father's bed. The sheets were just as Saro had turned them back.

There! There it was again! It sounded like singing. "Glory to God! On earth peace!"

Jamie breathed hard. Had he heard that? Or had he only said it to himself? He lay down again and pulled the quilts over his head.

"Get up, Jamie," he heard Father saying. "Put your clothes on quick."

Jamie opened his eyes. He saw daylight filling the room. He saw Father standing over him, bundled in warm clothes.

Wondering, Jamie flung the quilts back and rolled out of bed.

"Why Jamie," said Father, "you're already dressed!"

Father went to the stairs. "Saro! Honey!" he called. "Come quick!"

"What's happened, Father?" asked Saro.

"What are we going to do?" asked Honey as she fumbled sleepily with her shoelaces.

"Come with me," said Father.

"Where are we going?" asked Honey.

"To the stable?" asked Saro.

"The stable was no fit place," said Father. "Not when the church was close by, and it with a stove in it, and coal for burning."

Out into the cold, silent white morning they went. The wind had died. The clouds were lifting. One star in the vast sky, its brilliance fading in the growing light, shone down on Hurricane Gap.

Father led the way through the drifted snow. The others followed, stepping in his tracks. As Father pushed open the church door, the fragrance of the Christmas tree rushed out at them. The potbellied stove glowed red with the fire within.

Muffling his footsteps, Father walked quietly up the aisle. Wonderingly, the others followed. There, beside the starcrowned Christmas tree where the Christmas play was to have been given, they saw the woman. She lay on the old buffalo skin, covered with quilts. Beside her pallet sat the man.

The woman smiled at them. "You came to see?" she asked, and lifted the cover.

Saro went first and peeped under the cover. Honey went next.

"You look, too, Jamie," said Saro.

For a moment Jamie hesitated. He leaned forward and took one quick look. Then he turned, shot down the aisle and out of the church, slamming the door behind him.

Saro ran down the church aisle, calling after him.

"Wait, Saro," said Father, watching Jamie through he window.

To the house Jamie made his way, half running along the path Father's big boots had cut through the snowdrifts.

Inside the house he hurriedly pulled his shepherd's robe over his coat. He snatched up his crook from the chimney corner.

With his hand on the doorknob, he glanced toward the fireplace. There, under the mantel, hung Saro's and Honey's stockings. And there, beside them, hung his stocking! Now who had hung it there? It had in it the same bulge his stocking had had every Christmas morning since he could remember, a bulge made by an orange.

Jamie ran to the fireplace and felt the toe of his stocking. Yes, there was the dime, just as on other Christmas mornings.

Hurriedly, he emptied his stocking. With the orange and the dime in one hand and the crook in the other, he made his way toward the church. Father and Saro, still watching, saw his shepherd's robe—a spot of glowing color in a great white world.

Father opened the church door.

Without looking to the left or right, Jamie hurried up the aisle. Father and Saro followed him. Beside the pallet he dropped to his knees.

"Here is a Christmas gift for the Child," he said, clear and strong.

"Father!" gasped Saro. "Father, listen to Jamie!"

The woman turned back the covers from the baby's face. Jamie gently laid the orange beside the baby's tiny hand.

"And here's a gift for the Mother," Jamie said to the woman. He put the dime in her hand.

"Surely," the woman spoke softly, "the Lord lives this day."

"Surely," said Father, "the Lord does live this day, and all days. And He is loving and merciful and good."

In the hush that followed, Christmas in all its joys and its majesty, came to Hurricane Gap. And it wasn't so long ago at that. ✦

The Red Mittens

HARTLEY F. DAILEY

Old Man Riggs was the meanest and stingiest man in three counties—yet Linda wanted to give him mittens for Christmas!

Hartley F. Dailey was my very dear friend for many years—and he loved children. Of all the stories he wrote, this one about a stingy old man and a little girl named Linda is everyone's favorite. When asked about the origin of this story, Dailey wrote, "As to the Red Mittens story, I spent the years of my early adulthood in the Great Depression. If I write about that you can be sure I know what I am writing about. The character of Old Man Riggs was taken almost entirely from a man I knew a number of years before the story was written. . . . He was reputed to be a millionaire but the first time you met him you would have thought he was a pauper. The character of Jane was taken from my wife and Linda from my daughter, Nancy."

Hartley Dailey was born near Milton, West Virginia, in 1909. He never strayed far from there. In a reminiscent mood, in one of his last letters to me, he looked backward in time and concluded, "I believe my greatest accomplishment is to have married a good woman, who has been with me sixty-two years through good and bad. It hasn't been easy for her."

think I really count my Christmases from the year Linda was eight. That is the year when "Peace on earth, good will to men" first began to mean something to me.

That was in '34, the worst year of the Great Depression, at least for farmers. Like many another, I had bought a quarter section, 160 acres, just before the market crash, and at much too high a price. Now, with farm prices at rock bottom, the price of things we had to buy were rising. It took every cent we could scrape together just to pay the interest on the place.

That was the year we decided we just couldn't afford to buy Christmas presents. For ourselves—

Jane and I—we didn't mind, but for Linda, we felt differently. Our only child, she seemed almost a baby. She was a serious-minded little girl, with a wealth of silky brown hair, and a pair of enormous brown eyes, so warm they would have melted the heart of the legendary "Snow Queen." We felt she was just too young to understand why there was no money to buy presents.

There was a beautiful light-blue coat, just Linda's size, in the window of Lloyd's department store, in the county seat. Every time we'd go to town she'd go and stare into that store window to see if it was still there. But the price was an impossible $12.95! It might just as well have been a hundred. Jane went to great pains remaking a coat of her own, to fit Linda, and she wore it dutifully. But it could not take the place of the one in Lloyd's window.

In those days, our nearest neighbor was Old Man Riggs, whose 500 acres lay between our place and the river. Old Charley Riggs was the stingiest man in three counties, with a disposition like a sour apple, and an expression on his face that hinted his chief diet was unripe persimmons. He was reputed to have money, but you never would have guessed it. He dressed like a tramp, and he drove a broken-down old Model T. He never put side-curtains on it, no matter how cold the weather. He'd sit bolt upright, his big, knobby hands holding the steering wheel in a death-like grip. I never saw him wear a pair of gloves—not until after that Christmas.

One of the most pressing problems for a farmer in the hill country is WATER. If you don't have access to a spring or a stream, you must have deep wells to get it. And at that time, before electricity came to the hills, you pumped it by hand. And pumping all the water for all the animals on a farm is labor indeed.

I had been trying for years to negotiate a right-of-way across Old Man Riggs' place, to the river. Here I was, spending half my time pumping water, while across the narrowest point in Riggs' place, fifty yards from my pasture, was a whole river full! And it wasn't as if he needed it. He had over a mile of frontage—and he wouldn't sell me an inch!

As Christmas approached, Jane was busy going through the attic, picking out things to make, or

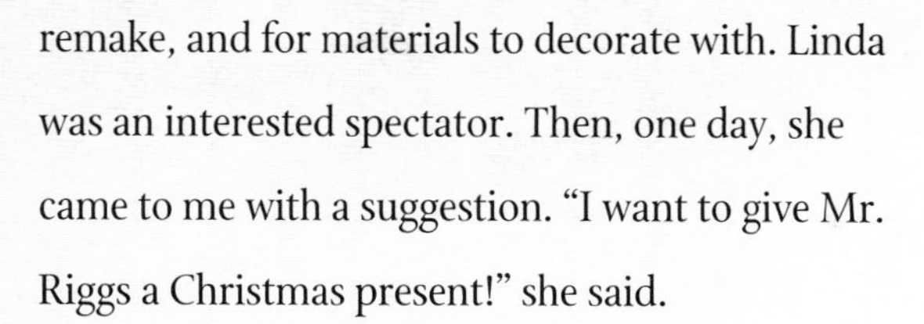

remake, and for materials to decorate with. Linda was an interested spectator. Then, one day, she came to me with a suggestion. "I want to give Mr. Riggs a Christmas present!" she said.

I was thunderstruck! But I said, "What could you give Mr. Riggs, Linda?"

"I'd have Mother make him some mittens, like she makes for you," came Linda's confident answer.

"Why," I blurted, "the old man would be too stingy to wear them, if you did."

I saw at once that I had made a mistake, for Linda hung her pretty head, and began making circles with her toe, in a way she had. "Mr. Riggs is my friend," she said. "He lets me eat pears from that big tree in his yard."

I wouldn't have been more surprised if she had said she had trained one of the local wild cats to catch mice in the kitchen. But, knowing her as I did, I shouldn't have been surprised, even at that. Myself, I wouldn't have given the old tightwad the time of day from his own watch, but I couldn't deny Linda anything, when she looked like that. Besides, I saw the hand of Jane in this, for Jane, the gentlest and sweetest of women, has an iron will that brooks no opposition in such matters. I went down on my knees beside Linda, and took her in my arms. "Aw, Honey," I told her, "if you want to give Mr. Riggs some mittens, you go right ahead!"

Every winter Jane made several pairs of zero-mittens for me. These were mittens cut from the best parts of my worn-out overalls, and lined with pieces of worn blankets. Then she would knit some cuffs of yarn, and sew them on.

These were the mittens Linda wanted to give to the old neighbor. Jane cut out two pairs for Old Man Riggs, but she left the sewing to Linda. She cut one pair from overalls, but she found an old skirt in the attic—I think the brightest red I ever saw—and she cut one pair from this. When they were finished, they went into a box, along with some of Jane's molasses cookies. Early on Christmas Eve, before dark, Linda took the box, and left it on Riggs' porch.

About eleven o'clock the next morning, my chores done, I was sitting in the living room, while Jane and Linda prepared our Christmas dinner. Suddenly, with a clatter like an earthquake in a tin shop, Old Man Riggs' Model T turned into our drive. He had his usual death grip on the wheel, but on his hands were the flaming red mittens!

He came to an abrupt halt just in front of the house, and climbed painfully to the ground. He